"Her love w...
like a butt...

Terzan continued bitterly, "Cilla couldn't wait to tell me that losing my sight relieved her of all obligations. Are you as weak as she is?"

"No!" Angie refuted fiercely, rubbing tears of shame from her eyes.

"Then prove it!" he challenged softly. "If you really are different from your sister, if you genuinely wish to make amends for her duplicity, then stay here and be the eyes with which I see, the hands with which I write."

Angie stumbled toward the door, too overwhelmed to speak, and halted on the threshold just long enough to heed his last command.

"Think about it, Miss Rose, and give me your decision tomorrow. If the situation I've outlined is too unconventional, I'd even be prepared to marry you."

MARGARET ROME

second-best bride

Harlequin Books

TORONTO • LONDON • LOS ANGELES • AMSTERDAM
SYDNEY • HAMBURG • PARIS • STOCKHOLM • ATHENS • TOKYO

Harlequin Presents edition published June 1981
ISBN 0-373-10438-3

Original hardcover edition published in 1981
by Mills & Boon Limited

CHAPTER ONE

'I don't understand!' Angie's perplexed grey eyes roved her sister's nonchalant expression, sensing instinctively that her air of bravado was merely a façade. 'If, as you say, you're afraid of this man—this Greek you met on holiday—why on earth did you agree to marry him?'

When Cilla's brilliant blue glance fell towards the carpet Angie's eyes widened. For the first time in years her younger sister was betraying signs of discomfiture—downcast head, shuffling feet, a slight tinge of colour on high cheekbones—all brought a vivid reminder of schooldays during which, in her role of protector, she had accepted punishment for Cilla's misdeeds and even managed to feel sympathy as she watched her squirming beneath the eye of a suspicious headmistress.

'Must you be so prim and prissy!' Typically, Cilla reacted with resentment to the slightest hint of criticism. 'I'm sick to death of listening to your lectures, fed up with being urged to act with propriety, to remember always to behave in a manner in keeping with Father's position. What position, for heaven's sake!' Irritably, she flung her arms wide to encompass the whole of the shabby sitting-room. 'Take a good look at our ancestral home,' she challenged, a scowl distorting her lovely features, and admit that it bears no comparison to the sort of place we ought to be living in. I'll never understand why a girl as beautiful as our late mother was said to have been, a girl brought up in a mansion and surrounded by luxury from birth, should have wasted her chances by marrying a penniless curate who, even in his youth, had not the slightest ambition to advance his station. Even today, twenty-five years on, he's merely the Reverend Philip Rose, tenant of the dilapidated vicarage of a poverty-stricken country parish!'

Appalled though she was by her sister's outburst, Angie managed to keep her voice steady when she told her simply:

'I imagine Mother would have found it supremely easy to fall in love with our very lovable father.'

For a second there was silence, then suddenly Cilla's tense body crumpled into Angie's arms.

'I'm sorry,' she sobbed through tempestuous tears, 'honestly, I didn't mean a word I said, no one knows better than I do that we've been blessed with the sweetest-natured, most charitable, loving, generous father in the whole world! I don't know why . . . how *could* I speak of him in such a way . . .'

'You're overwrought.' After a swift, forgiving hug, Angie pushed her on to a nearby couch and sat down beside her. 'It's not like you to give way to tears,' she admonished mildly. 'For the past couple of years your life has been filled with fun and activity; I could have sworn you'd forgotten how to cry. But I suspect your mysterious Greek is in some way responsible for the sudden storm, therefore, as I've heard only the bare bones of the story, you'd better begin at the beginning and fill me in.'

Cilla did not immediately respond to her request, but knowing that she needed time to recover her composure Angie did not press her but sat quietly waiting until her sister was ready to explain her uncharacteristic loss of control.

She strove for a look of serenity, but beneath her calm exterior she was worried and not a little surprised by her sister's storm of resentment. Though still not quite twenty, Cilla had seemed to achieve sophistication overnight. Immediately after leaving school she had scorned the chore of parish routine in favour of the good life, being escorted to dances and dinners by the legion of young men she had met during her numerous visits to the homes of wealthy relatives.

Angie had always declined such invitations herself, not because of any feeling of inferiority, but because the family budget had been stretched to the limit providing sufficient outfits to ensure that Cilla might hold her own in the midst of her wealthy friends.

Her eyes kindled with appreciation as she scanned her sister's vivacious beauty, then sharpened with anxiety when she glimpsed white teeth chewing a trembling bottom lip.

'I'm waiting, Cilla,' she encouraged gently. 'I've

never known you so reluctant to share a confidence.'

'You're going to be angry with me,' Cilla gulped.

'I'll try not to be,' Angie promised, a twinkle belying the solemnity of her expression. Even as a child, Cilla had shown a propensity for drama.

After struggling for some minutes to find words, Cilla began with a shamefaced apology. 'I suppose it was wrong of me to keep you and Father in the dark about my engagement, but to be honest,' she gulped, 'once I returned home it seemed to become more and more unreal—a dreamy interval, thrilling while it lasted, but so swift and intransient it became easy to believe it had never happened in reality.'

'I assume,' Angie prodded gently when Cilla seemed to be in danger of lapsing back into her dream world, 'that the event took place during your holiday on Cousin Freddie's yacht?'

She nodded. 'We were cruising in the Aegean when a sudden storm made it imperative for us to reach some kind of harbour. The nearest land was an island, a tiny gem of a place, which we discovered was owned by a wealthy Greek, Terzan Helios, who used it as a retreat from the pressures of the business world.'

'Such wealth seems almost sinful,' commented Angie, who could be impressed by the ownership of an allotment.

Cilla's head jerked up to eye her sister with respect. 'The word is very apt—Terzan *is* sinful, sinfully wealthy, sinfully handsome and,' her voice trembled, 'wickedly attractive.'

Angie's breath caught in a sharp gasp. Cilla might have been describing the devil! Immediately, her mind became stamped with an impression of a dark Greek head sprouting horns. She clenched her hands and found to her surprise that her palms were sweating, but she could not spare the time to wonder when Cilla continued:

'In the manner of all Greeks, he was wonderfully hospitable. He insisted upon accommodating all ten of us, passengers and crew, in his home and pressed us to remain long after the storm had blown itself out. We were his guests for a month,' she admitted, sounding as surprised as Angie felt, 'and even Freddie was impressed by the lavishness of our host's hospitality. I suppose that might account for the way he chivvied me into egging him on when,' she hesitated, colour rising slowly in her cheeks, 'it became evident to everyone that Terzan was smitten with me.'

Feeling an urge to vent a puzzling inner anger against someone—anyone—Angie exploded. 'If that isn't typical of the Honourable Freddie! It puzzles me why you bother to cultivate his friendship. I'm sorry to have to say this about a close relative, but in my opinion that young man is a weak degenerate, spoiled from birth by doting parents and a far too lavish income!'

'You two have never hit it off,' Cilla almost smiled. 'If only you wouldn't rise too easily to his teasing, he wouldn't bother to enquire after your

Brownie pack at each moment of meeting.'

'He doesn't enquire, he sneers!' Angie corrected, quietly fuming. 'I admit that I spend most of my time helping around the parish, but by no means do I deserve the title "Goody Two-Shoes" that he so sarcastically bestowed upon me.'

Cilla shrugged, her mind occupied with more important issues. 'You still haven't answered my question,' she pointed out, her voice strained. 'Will you go to Karios and explain to Terzan why I can't marry him?'

As it had when the question had first been broached, Angie's blood ran suddenly cold. For the first time in her life she suffered panic, a sensation so strange she sought refuge in prevarication.

'How can I be expected to explain a situation I don't understand myself?' she husked. 'Though it's beyond me to comprehend how, you have admitted that in the space of a few short weeks this Greek managed to convince you that you wanted nothing more than to spend the rest of your life with him, yet now, barely six months later, you claim that attraction has turned into fear. How come?' she frowned. 'You haven't seen him since you left his island, so how has he managed to communicate fear?'

'In the beginning,' Cilla jerked, 'we talked on the telephone almost every day, then for about six weeks I heard nothing from him. It was during that time of silence that I began to realise what a mistake I'd made, and as the weeks went past with no further word from him I began to hope that he, too, had put our relationship into perspective, that he was regarding the interlude as nothing more than a light flirtation that had achieved unwarranted importance with the help of conducive surroundings.'

'I understand,' Angie nodded. And she did understand. Although such a frivolous outlook was alien to her own nature, she knew that to Cilla such reasoning was normal. 'Then what happened,' she prompted, 'obviously, he surprised you by once more getting in touch?'

'Yes, by letter,' Cilla nodded miserably, 'a shower of letters that developed into a storm once I told him I had no intention of marrying him.'

'He must love you very much,' Angie pondered sadly, feeling fleeting pity for the rejected Greek, 'nevertheless, though an engagement implies commitment it's by no means binding, a girl is entitled to change her mind—and also to expect her fiancé, if he has any pretensions towards being a gentleman, to accept his dismissal with dignity.'

'Terzan is no gentleman.' Her sister shivered violently. 'He's very much an uncut diamond, rich but ruthless, outwardly sophisticated yet uncivilised enough to use caveman tactics to force me to keep my word. That's why, suspecting that he might arrive on the doorstep any minute, I sent a message promising to return to Karios as soon as possible. I *had* to, Angie, I was desperate to keep him at bay!' Suddenly, a shy smile appeared on her lips and her voice dropped almost to a whisper.

'You see, I've fallen in love—and this time it's for real . . .'

'You have?' Angie gasped. 'With whom . . .?'

'With David Montgomery—and if my instinct serves me right he's almost on the verge of proposing.'

Angie's eyes lit up. 'That's wonderful news,' she beamed. 'I'm so pleased for you, darling. I've always liked David, he's so steady and dependable, by far the nicest person amongst your crowd of giddy friends.'

'That's all very well, but his father is a viscount!' Cilla's voice rose high with panic. 'If his parents should hear the merest whisper about my engagement to Terzan Helios they'll be bound to oppose our marriage!'

'Oh, heavens!' Angie sank back against the couch, exhausted by a gamut of emotions. 'You do make life complicated . . .'

'I won't in future, I *promise*.' Cilla leant closer to plead. 'Please, Angie, take this back to Karios for me, place it personally in the hands of that tyrannical Greek to prove to him that our engagement is definitely over. You *can't* refuse! My future happiness depends upon his remaining on Karios and out of my life!'

She jumped to her feet and flung out of the room, leaving Angie staring at the huge diamond ring that had been dropped into her palm. Transfixed with awe, she raised her hand higher, then jerked with revulsion when a stray shaft of sunlight pierced the stony heart, firing into life a brilliant, baleful glare.

Carefully she stretched out a trembling hand to place the ring upon a nearby table. Averting her eyes from its magnificence, her mind from its cost, she sat still as a statue, striving to regain control over trembling limbs and chaotic thoughts.

'That's an old and well-tried trick of yours, my girl,' silently she berated her absent sister, 'dumping a problem in my lap, then running hell for leather out of earshot of a refusal! But it isn't going to work this time. You've swum too far out of my depth and I've no intention of being drowned, on your behalf, in the depths of the Aegean Sea!'

Cilla was still absent when Angie joined her father at the dinner table. As she took her place next to him, she missed his usual beam of welcome and cast an anxious glance as she served him with his soup.

'Had a good day, Father?' she enquired, determinedly bright.

'So-so . . .!' he sighed, and began heavily seasoning his soup.

'That's pepper,' she pointed out, knowing he had no great liking for it.

'Oh, dear!' If he had been a man accustomed to using expletives, she felt certain he would have sworn. As it was, he relieved his feelings by pushing his plate aside with the irritable comment, 'I'm not very hungry this evening, I'll skip this course, if you don't mind.'

Wondering if her quiet, placid world was to continue permanently topsy-turvy, Angie waded doggedly through the soup it had taken her all afternoon to prepare and left him to his brooding. Normally, she would not have hesitated to enquire about whatever it was that was troubling him, but her mind was so full of her own worries she did not feel inclined to overburden it with such problems as how to secure the services of a chiropodist willing to visit the isolated village once a month simply to trim pensioners' toenails, or how to discover the vandal within the Boy Scouts' troop who had carved his initials upon the church hall door.

But when they had reached the sweet course and her father had not spoken one word, she realised that he was not merely worried but deeply disturbed.

'Where's Cilla?' The sharpness of his tone caused her to jump.

'I don't know, she left the house a couple of hours ago, but I can ring around, if you like, and try to trace her whereabouts.'

'No matter, upon reflection perhaps it might be better if I have a cooling off period before speaking to that young woman.'

She found his tone, his whole attitude, startling. Although he would have been most upset if anyone had accused him of favouritism, over the years he had betrayed in many small ways that Cilla, the daughter who had inherited her mother's beauty, was the apple of his eye. Rarely had she been scolded, never had she been denied anything it had been in his power to provide—especially since the death of his wife.

'Why? What's she done wrong?' Blank amazement echoed in her query.

Once again her father pushed aside his plate with the food untouched. He looked pained, as if he was finding it difficult to confide even in Angie who was used to sharing all his confidences.

'The Bishop telephoned me this afternoon to arrange a meeting,' he clamped. 'At first he was cagey about the subject he wanted to discuss, but because he's an old friend, and because he has known you two girls since birth, he finally admitted that he'd received a complaint from one of my parishioners concerning Cilla's conduct.'

'Oh, *Father* . . .!' Angie jumped to her feet, outraged. 'The Bishop must be aware that every parish has at least one scandalmonger in its midst, one warped mind that condemns every youthful prank as evil! I'm disappointed in the Bishop, I'd never have believed him capable of listening to gossip, much less acting upon it!'

'*Sit down*, Angie, and kindly allow me to finish!'

The command was voiced with such unusual sternness that in spite of her indignation she obeyed immediately, slumping into her chair with a force that was far from elegant.

'Whatever the Bishop's personal views,' her father continued, 'he's honour bound to follow up any complaint. He made it quite plain that he considered the charge frivolous, then followed that up by stressing that even if it were not, the behaviour of any member of my family could never be allowed to cast a reflection upon my work. Nevertheless,' he sighed heavily and brushed a hand across his eyes, betraying an attitude of such deep dejection Angie could cheerfully have wrung her sister's neck, 'I must take some of the blame, for I fear I've allowed her to become spoiled.'

'Of course you haven't!'

'Yes, my dear,' he insisted firmly, 'and also, during the process, I've closed my eyes to the fact that you've become the parish dogsbody, the one who does all the work and reaps none of the pleasure.'

'But my work *is* a pleasure!' she insisted fiercely, his distress bringing her close to tears. 'And besides that, Cilla is so young and beautiful she deserves to have fun.'

'She's a mere two years younger than yourself,' he pointed out sternly, 'and also you're a very pretty reflection of your sister.'

The thoughtless comparison would once have hurt, but over the years Angie had become resigned to living in the shadow of Cilla's beauty, could now accept without rancour that although they both possessed the same delicate bone structure, the same clear skin, and were almost identical in build and height, Cilla's hair glowed sun-bright whereas her own had the pale lustre of moonlight; Cilla's eyes were a vivid, unclouded blue whereas hers were a solemn grey. Also, it was a constant source of annoyance that the clothes Cilla discarded immediately they became unfashionable hung like shapeless bags around her own much less rounded frame.

Her father stood erect and squared his shoulders. 'I've decided that I must forbid Cilla further prolonged visits to the homes of your mother's relatives. Too much luxurious living and the dubious example set by your pleasure-seeking cousins, especially young Freddie, has made her wayward.'

'For heaven's sake, Father!' she stared aghast, 'of what exactly has she been accused?'

'Of waking the entire neighbourhood by racing through country lanes in noisy sports cars; of disrupting the peace and quiet of the village pub with noisy drinking parties, and of being extremely impudent to elders who attempted to remonstrate with her,' he spelled out with obvious distaste.

Numb with disbelief, Angie watched his stiff figure retreating from the dining-room, uncertain whether to give in to frustrated tears or to howls of derisory laughter. With sudden insight she was seeing her father and his contemporaries through Cilla's eyes, and deep sympathy welled for the girl condemned as delinquent simply because of youthful high spirits.

But like most men slow to be moved to anger, her father, once roused, could be formidable—for the sake of Cilla's future happiness *he must never be allowed to find out about the Greek!*

CHAPTER TWO

As Angie sat in the stern of a motorboat that was speeding her across the bluest water she had ever seen, she shivered and pulled the collar of her coat closer around her neck, glad that she had paid no heed to Cilla's insistence that it was too shabby to be worn even for travelling and that in any case it would not be needed once she reached the land where flowers bloomed all the year round and where trees would be hanging heavy with citrus fruit, splashing hot colour against a background of spring green.

Unfortunately, as Nikos, the manservant who had been sent to meet her, had haltingly explained, conditions throughout the islands could be as unpredictable as the nature of the Greek himself, which was why the sun was sulking behind cloud, the sea tossed with temper and darkly frowning.

As he threaded the craft past many small islands that loomed in the distance and then quickly faded into mists astern, Nikos cast anxious glances at the pale-faced *Anghlika* who seemed oblivious to sporting dolphins and to the shoals of fish streaking silver through a wine-dark sea. Mercifully, she also seemed immune to waves so rough they had been known to force spicy oaths and hasty prayers from the lips of land-loving peasants.

Unaware of his speculative eyes, Angie sat hugged in misery, painfully aware, as a patient becomes aware of the slowly receding effects of anaesthetic, that she had been manipulated. The speed with which she had been coaxed, cajoled, then finally hustled on her way to Karios had left her no time for argument, no opportunity to air her doubts about the wisdom of presenting herself before Terzan Helios as a mediator in place of the fiancée he was expecting.

She had been a fool to allow herself to be forced into coming! Yet Cilla had left her with no alternative. Was it really only two days since the dreadful row that had threatened to tear her small family apart?

Even now she could hear her father's voice, ringing unfamiliar in anger, indicting Cilla with selfishness, frivolity, and utter disregard for the feelings of others. At first Cilla had reacted with defiance, had even threatened to leave home for good unless she were allowed to live her life as she wanted to and not in accordance with the wishes of her father's parishioners. Only his cold reminder that she had no talent for work, no means of supporting herself, had seemed to bring her to her senses.

Angie had suspected, then immediately wiped the uncharitable thought from her mind, that Cilla's sudden capitulation had not been motivated by remorse but had been a bid for time, time to enable David Montgomery to propose, to transplant her from poverty to luxury, from the obscurity of a country vicarage into the realms of titled society.

Her father, however, had been completely won over by eyes of tearful blue that had pleaded mutely for forgiveness, and by the sobs that had racked her slender frame when she had flung herself into his arms and begged, 'I will behave in future, Father, I promise! Everything you've said is true, I've been selfishly unfair to you and Angie, but I'll try as hard as I know how to make up for my thoughtlessness.' At the sight of his dawning smile she had glistened as if suddenly inspired. 'I have an idea! Only this afternoon Angie was telling me how much she yearned to be able to take a holiday, to escape the ties of the parish and enjoy a first taste of freedom—let her go, Father, and let me take over her duties, that way I can discharge my debt to both of you and might even manage to mollify the feelings of any parishioners I may have offended!'

Angie winced as she recalled the look of hurt surprise her father had cast across Cilla's shoulder. He would never know what it had cost her to bite back hot words of denial that had sprung to her lips, or to simulate delighted astonishment when the very next day Cilla had triumphantly announced that by telephoning influential friends she had managed to reserve a seat on a plane leaving for Greece that very night.

'Is the young *Anghlika* not feeling well?'

When Nikos' swarthy features swam into focus she realised with a start that the boat had been moored alongside a jetty centred within a wild, romantic bay ringed with boulder-strewn cliffs upon which cypresses stood sentinel-stiff and vivid poppies ran like streams of lava towards the sea.

'I'm fine, thank you.' Her apprehensive eyes ran the length of the cliff. 'Just a little tired. Have we much farther to go?'

Laughter boomed from the burly Greek manservant who, even on such short acquaintance, had impressed her with his air of uncalculating kindness.

'You are thinking you will need the stamina of a mountain goat to scale that cliff, eh?' His dark head nodded upwards. 'Don't worry,' he grinned, 'in less than five minutes you will be in the presence of the *kirios*.'

Though his voice, whenever he spoke of his boss, echoed with pride and affection, her dread increased as he led her towards a lift built into the cliffside, then demonstrated with the press of a button how wealth could smooth a path through even the most rugged terrain.

This fact was further demonstrated when she stepped out of the lift just as the sun broke through cloud, giving an impression of stepping into another world, a world of closely-shaven lawns kept fresh and green with the aid of lazily turning sprinklers; of flowering shrubs, showers of mimosa; clumps of waist-high geraniums, tall marguerites, lilies, tulips, and masses of blue campanula festooning low rocky walls. Sun-baked paths fanned in the direction of a white-walled villa, its red tiled roof overlapping to form a terrace trap of welcoming shade.

'You like?' Nikos beamed. 'Inside, we have central heating, running water, and many beautiful bathrooms.'

Angie smiled, and for the first time found the courage to seek an answer to the question that had been worrying her ever since Nikos had met her at the airport. He had been instructed to pick up Miss Rose to act as her escort for the remainder of the journey, yet his expression had remained impassive when she had appeared, even though he must have been expecting Cilla.

'Why didn't your employer come to the airport himself? After all, he was expecting the arrival of his fiancée.'

A shadow clouded Nikos' face. He hesitated, then shrugged. 'There are days when the *kirios* feels no inclination to travel.' The admission seemed dragged past his lips.

'Are you saying that he couldn't be *bothered*?' she queried indignantly.

Resentful colour rose high in his cheeks, for one terrifying second he looked angry enough to bite, but then he mastered his emotions sufficiently to reply. 'I am saying that a man needs to cling fast to his pride. Unfortunately, 'his voice dropped to a puzzling whisper, 'the taller the bamboo, the lower it can be forced to bend.'

As she followed Nikos towards the entrance to the villa Angie heard the strains of a *bouzoukia* in the far distance. Her footsteps faltered as something deep inside her stirred in response to the haunting yet wildly passionate music being plucked from the heartstrings of the Greek violin. The sound, new and different to her ears, made her forcibly aware that she had been transplanted into alien soil, into a land whose sun-baked earth could shrivel tender roots, amongst people whose pride and passion were inherited from legendary ancestors—from Zeus, Lord of Heaven and Prince of Light; from Apollo, the sun-god who could destroy as well as give life; from Ares, the god who loved to go to war, and from Eros, the handsome, blindfolded god of desire and passion who was said to have whetted with blood the grindstone on which he sharpened his arrows.

The interior of the villa seemed lined with marble, white, pink, black and veined, filling the shadowed hall with the cool atmosphere of a tomb. Angie shivered and tightened the belt around her waist to combat a sensation of icy fingertips stroking the length of her spine as she followed in Nikos' wake, her heels tapping, fast as her heartbeats, against the black marble floor and upon each tread of a milk-white staircase hewn from the same imposing stone.

It was a relief, when Nikos flung open a door and stepped aside inviting her to enter, to discover that the room she had been given looked far less austere. Though the windows were shuttered to keep out the heat of the sun, shell pink drapes with a matching bedcover, lightwood furniture, and an expanse of creamy, curled-fleece rug bestowed an aura of feminine appeal.

'I guessed that you would welcome an opportunity to freshen up before your meeting with the *kirios*,' the thoughtful Nikos grinned, depositing her one insignificant suitcase beside the bed. 'My wife, Crisulla, who acts as housekeeper, will send a girl to unpack for you, please inform her if there is anything you need. Meanwhile, I'll tell the *kirios* that you have arrived.'

Even when the door had closed behind him she found it impossible to relax. Though air-conditioned, the room was pleasantly warm, yet her fingers felt stiff with cold as she fumbled with the buttons on her coat before tossing it on to the bed. Behind a door that Nikos had indicated she found a bathroom, a sea green grotto with bath, basin and shower served by water that gushed from the mouths of gold-plated dolphins. Crystal jars filled with an assortment of oils and bath essences were ranged on a shelf next to a deep recess piled high with cream and green layers of luxurious bath towels.

She took a startled step backwards, thinking she had seen a ghost, then realised with a nervous giggle that it was her own frightened face she saw reflected in a mirror. Averting her eyes from the pale, pinched oval, she bent over the basin to bathe her face with cool water, then guiltily dabbed it dry on one corner of a pristine towel.

She was trying, without much success, to flatten the worst of the creases in her skirt when a rap upon the door warned her that Nikos had returned to escort her into the presence of his boss.

'Just a second!' she quavered, rushing to the dressing table to run a comb through her hair, but her hands were trembling so much she threw down the comb in despair before berating her mirrored image.

'You're merely here to deliver a message, remember! Not a pleasant message, admittedly, nevertheless there's no need to be so ridiculously scared, for however violently the Greek may react you have the consolation of knowing that by this time tomorrow you'll be on your way home.'

Looking unflappable as a schoolmarm in her neat woollen skirt and prim white blouse, she stepped outside into the passageway, steeled to carry out the most unpleasant task she had ever been called upon to perform. Nikos smiled approval, then, obviously anxious not to keep his boss waiting, he guided her along the passageway, down the staircase, then across the width of black marble floor. He halted outside a door at the far end of the hall, tapped once upon its panel, then, in response to a command from within, he opened the door and stood back, indicating that she should go inside.

After a deep, steadying breath she obeyed, then felt deserted, stranded upon a sea of carpet, when the door closed with a thud behind her.

The darkness inside the room, and also throughout the villa, seemed markedly contradictory to the nature of the sun-loving Greeks and as she groped her way forward she wondered at its owner's obvious aversion to rays of sunshine dammed up outside of tightly-closed shutters.

'Priscilla ...?' Her sister's name, uttered in a slightly accented voice traced with enquiry, brought her to a sudden halt. As she sensed movement, her eyes swivelled in the direction of an armchair and saw a figure uncoiling from its depths to stand magnificently erect—broad shoulders tapering towards narrow hips; lean thighs, and long legs set astride, in a manner that unearthed from her memory a quotation from her schooldays.

'He doth bestride the narrow world.

Like a Colossus.'

'I did you an injustice, *agape mou*,' he continued, his lips twisted into a slightly bitter smile, 'I did not believe for one moment that you would come.'

Angie stared speechless at the tall Greek whose eyes lurked, unreadable, behind dark glasses. But his shock of black hair, the lean planes of his face—deeply tanned, yet in some indefinable way lacking Nikos' bloom of vitality—his tight, snarl-edged smile, his chiselled profile, fitted her preconceived image perfectly—except for the omission of the horns.

'Well, why don't you speak?' His voice developed a sudden edge. 'We have been parted too long, have you no welcoming kiss for your fiancé?'

She stifled a small gasp of amazement, then realised immediately that the dimness of the room, together with her superficial likeness to Cilla, could account for his mistaking her identity.

'Cilla—Priscilla couldn't come,' she husked, daring a tentative step forward, 'so she sent me to deliver her explanation.'

'*Who are you?*'

She cowered from his anger, reminded more than ever of a powerful Colossus.

'I'm Angie—Angelina—Priscilla's sister,' she gasped, despising her own cowardice yet unable for the life of her to control her trembling. She imagined she could feel his stare boring through dense glasses and winced from the understandable anger that exploded into his words.

'How very appropriate,' he sneered. 'As Priscilla's talents are purely physical, I must assume that it was pure chance rather than deliberate design that prompted her to choose as her go-between one who shares her name with angels who carried messages to man from God. Very well, Angelina,' he grated, 'though I've already guessed its content, you had better do your duty by delivering whatever message you bring from the goddess Priscilla.'

Distaste for her task increased a thousandfold as she recognised heartache and disappointment behind his bitter sarcasm. He had not moved a muscle from the moment she had made herself known, had not led her to a seat nor made any of the polite gestures a visitor is entitled to expect of a host, yet she had been prepared to overlook these omissions until he shocked her by resuming his seat, leaving her standing humble as a servant awaiting the instructions of her master.

'*The man's an uncivilised boor,*' she fumed, '*totally devoid of social graces. Cilla's well rid of him!*'

The knowledge gave her courage and steadied her tone to the point of coolness.

'My sister has changed her mind, she has no wish to come to Karios because she has fallen in love with someone else. Indeed, she is expecting to be married very shortly,' she told him with an utter lack of compunction. 'In the circumstances, she would be grateful if you would kindly stop pestering—threatening—her with visits that would be embarrassing to you both. She also asked me to return this.' She thrust forward a hand with the huge diamond glistening in her palm, but to her surprise he made no effort to take it, did not react at all, not even when she waved it under his nose.

'Please have the courtesy to accept my sister's decision as final,' in spite of herself she began to plead. 'I know you feel resentful that she didn't come in person to explain her feelings, but you more than anyone must know how tender-hearted she is, how reluctant to inflict hurt. This ring belongs to you—please take it . . .'

Violently, he jerked forward so that her hand came in contact with his chest, sending the ring spinning to the floor.

'Now look what you've done!' she flared. 'Well, you'll have to search for it yourself, because I've certainly no intention of scrabbling on the floor!'

'Then it must remain where it is, Miss Rose,' he clenched, 'for I think the sister whom you hold in such high esteem must have omitted to inform you that I am blind.'

CHAPTER THREE

'The *kirios's* blindness is the result of an accident,' Nikos replied to Angie's frantic query, long after Terzan Helios had dismissed her from his presence. He had kicked her out, metaphorically speaking, but not until after he had made plain the contempt he felt for Cilla and his dislike of herself.

'The great love of his life was motor racing,' Nikos continued mournfully, 'it was his antidote against the restrictions imposed upon his freedom by the endless board meetings that are an integral part of big business. But once he was seated behind the wheel of a powerful racing car, competing against professionals whose skill was no greater than his own, he became carefree and relaxed, each race acting upon him like a tonic, so physically and mentally rejuvenating that he was able to return with enthusiasm to the business arena.'

'How did the accident happen?' She shivered, chilled to the bone since Terzan's shock announcement.

He shrugged angrily. 'In the manner that such accidents usually happen in that dangerous sport,' he almost spat. 'It is not enough for a man to be a skilled driver, to have nerves of steel, to have the finest car that money can buy, because invariably it is one of the lesser skilled, driving a machine

30

that is less than perfect, who is the source of trouble—as was so in this case. A car driven by a young, inexperienced driver spun out of control causing a pile-up. The *kirios* was not involved, but he jumped from his car to go to the assistance of the young man who was trapped. When he was mere yards away from it the car exploded. The miracle is that he was not killed, that the only damage he suffered was to his sight. If only he had listened to my warnings!' Nikos's misery was such he sank down into a chair and buried his face in his hands. 'That blindness should be inflicted upon anyone is bad enough, but the world cannot afford to lose the talents of a man such as the *kirios*!'

Angie's pity was so great she wanted to join in his weeping, but one important question remained to be asked, one traitorous doubt that had to be erased from her mind.

'When ... when did the accident occur? Was it before or after my sister's arrival in Karios?'

'Why, afterwards, of course!' He raised his head, his expression bewildered. 'It was widely reported in the press because of the human interest angle, I suppose, the added poignancy of the blinded driver having just recently become betrothed.'

Shock turned into frozen horror. Long after Nikos had left her Angie remained huddled in a chair staring sightlessly out of a window, wrestling with the enormity of Cilla's selfishness, the lack of conscience that had allowed her to use her sister as a buffer between herself and a man's justifiable anger, the utter callousness with which she had deserted her fiancé at the time when he needed her most.

At intervals during her trance tears intruded, tears of shame on Cilla's behalf, tears of pity for the virile, ambitious man trapped inside a cage of blindness, a man who faltered where once he had strode; who fumbled for what once he had snatched; who had to accept help when it had been his custom to give, who was used to roaming the world, but who was now incarcerated inside a villa where the sun could not aggravate the eyes of a hunter—now hunted.

She reacted with a start to the sound of a tap upon her door.

'Come in!' she husked, then cleared her throat and called again, a little louder.

A young girl responded by stepping inside the room and half-bobbing a curtsey. '*Kalispera*,' she greeted shyly. 'My name is Lira, and I've been sent to help you unpack.'

'Thank you, Lira.' Angie managed to smile through her misery. 'But there's no need, my night-dress and toothbrush are all I require and they're in my small overnight case.'

'Oh, but . . .' Lira began a protest, then hesitated with a confused blush.

'Yes, what is it?' Angie sensed exactly how the tonguetied girl was feeling. 'Please don't be shy,' she smiled, 'tell me . . .?'

'It is just that the *kirios* is expecting you to join him for dinner,' she burst out, 'and when I saw him he was looking rather ... impatient,' she gasped, then clasped a hand over her mouth as if amazed by her own temerity.

But she could not have felt half so amazed as Angie. 'The *kirios* is waiting for me?' Astonishment propelled her to her feet. 'But I never dreamt . . .!' Her panic-stricken eyes swept the room searching for inspiration—how to react, what to say, *what to wear*! Then like a douche of icy water came the realisation that it did not matter, that if she were to go downstairs to dinner wearing nothing at all he would have no way of knowing.

The fact that he could bear to be in her company at all was encouraging. More than anything she yearned for an opportunity to outline her own part in the drama, to explain that had she been in possession of the true facts she would not have broken the news of Cilla's defection in such a heartless manner.

She ran into the bathroom to splash away all traces of tears, then, resigned to the fact that she had no time to change, hesitated just long enough to run a comb through her hair before rushing out of the room towards the stairs.

Crisulla was making her way across the hall carrying a serving dish with a domed silver cover. She could not speak English, but managed to convey, by way of smiles and nods, that she was making her way to the dining-room. So Angie followed slowly in her wake, giving herself time to control the panting caused by her headlong rush downstairs.

Terzan Helios was already seated at the table with Nikos in attendance, and her heart swelled almost to bursting point when she detected embarrassment in his caustic observation.

'Thank you for joining me, Miss Rose. As this will be the first time I have dined with a companion since losing my sight I must ask you to make allowances if my tie should happen to dangle in my soup.'

Nikos cast a sympathetic glance over her flushed cheeks as he served her, before retracing his steps to stand hovering like a guardian angel behind his master's chair.

Angie found it harder than anything she had ever done in her life before to force spoonsful of soup down a throat aching with unshed tears, trying hard not to look, but feeling her eyes drawn as if hypnotised towards the head of the table, willing the proud, dark Greek to avoid any mishap as slowly and carefully he progressed through the first course until his plate was almost empty.

Her relief was so great when Nikos removed his plate that she felt like applauding, but then she was once more cast into the depth of pity when he moved his head directly beneath the beam of an overhead lamp and she saw that his brow was beaded with the sweat of tense endeavour.

'Your arrival is most opportune, Miss Rose.' The steadiness of his voice seemed to make nonsense of her judgment.

'It is . . .?' She managed to croak out the query.

'Yes, indeed,' he nodded. 'As I have no wish to

spend the rest of my life as a hermit, I must re-train before resuming my place in society. An essential part of that re-training is to achieve sufficient confidence to eat in the presence of others, and as I have no wish to inflict my failings upon friends I need a guinea-pig on whom to practise—someone whose opinion is of no consequence.'

Angie weathered the insult with a calm he seemed to find infuriating, thereby strengthening her suspicion that his choice of words had been deliberate—symptomatic of the hurt inflicted by her sister. Understanding the motivation behind his hurtful remarks made them so much easier to bear that she found herself able to enjoy the remainder of the meal—simple dishes of grilled fish and meat roasted on the spit, cooked by Crisulla in a characteristically Greek fashion.

Feeling the meal should not pass without comment, she shyly addressed Nikos. 'Your wife is a superb cook, Nikos, please tell her that I'm most impressed by my first encounter with Greek cuisine.'

A beam of appreciation spread across Nikos's face, but it was his master who replied with sour lack of grace.

'Greeks are noted for their simplicity of living, nevertheless, they consider cooking an art and a superlative cook such as Crisulla a genius. The English, however, place a higher importance upon their surroundings than upon the food that is served to them, they will go hungry in order to preserve gentility, consequently most other nationalities view their opinion on higher matters with great suspicion.'

When the meal was finished they retired to a small sitting-room where, once Nikos had served her with coffee and then ensured that a tray containing a decanter of brandy, a silver box filled with cheroots, and a table lighter were in easy reach of his master's chair, he withdrew, leaving them alone together.

Angie sipped her coffee, unaware that her knuckles were whitening under the pressure of her grip upon the tiny cup, as she followed each one of Terzan's careful, deliberate movements. She ached to offer assistance, yet some instinct warned her not to interfere when his lean brown fingers groped for the lid of the box, then fumbled inside in search of a cheroot. But when he clenched one between his teeth and then began guiding the lighter towards its tip she jumped to her feet, afraid for his safety.

'Let me light it for you!'

'No, thank you,' he refused tersely, 'I can manage.'

'Oh, but . . .'

The lighter flared, searing the objection on her lips.

'I am almost a professional blind man now, Miss Rose.' He leant back and took an exaggerated puff at his cheroot. 'I learnt this trick many weeks ago when I was lying in hospital with my eyes bandaged. At first, I scorched my fingers, once I even burnt the bedcovers—to the fury of the nurse in charge—but now I'm perfectly competent.'

Realising that he needed to assert his independence in every way possible, Angie swallowed hard and dropped back into her chair.

'You are very brave,' she faltered, her heart so full she found it difficult to speak.

His dark head swivelled in the direction of her voice, his glowering look, the bitter twist of his lips, indicating that for some reason her words had angered him.

'If you must feel pity, Miss Rose, then for God's sake keep it to yourself! And please, never make the mistake of thinking me calm simply because I insist upon doing small, insignificant tasks for myself, of thinking me resigned to living the rest of my life without being able to see! I will never come to terms with the humiliation of having my meat cut into manageable pieces; of having to identify each item on my plate in relation to the hands on a clock—potatoes at three o'clock, vegetables at six—a device dreamt up by Nikos to save me the indignity of having to be spoonfed. Bravery implies a nobility of character that I do not possess. I've discovered an inner strength, that's true, but it is a strength drawn from vices rather than from virtues, from obstinacy, aggressiveness, and from having too large a share of the Greek's insatiable thirst for independence.'

He flicked his cheroot with a force that scattered ash all over a beautiful, pastel-coloured rug, but Angie dared not protest, hardly dared even to breath as he continued to blister:

'Some day I mean to resume my place in society, but before I do so I must accept the fact that until I become accustomed to being blind I must rely upon the help of others. In other words, I must learn to be patient, and believe me, Miss Rose, until you arrived I had no idea how very difficult that might turn out to be!'

He must have heard her stifled gasp, must have known how hurtful his cruel words would sound, yet his expression did not soften, not even when she trembled a dignified apology.

'I'm sorry. If my presence upsets you so much I'd better leave.'

'No!' When the rustle of her skirt betrayed her intention to flee he clamped out the command. 'Sit down—I'll let you know when I'm ready to be left alone!'

Not doubting his promise for one moment, she almost fell into her chair and clasped her hands around trembling knees. Only the faintest of sounds had betrayed her movement, yet he relaxed, satisfied that she had obeyed, then surprised her by offering:

'Would you like a drink?'

'No . . . no, thank you,' she quivered, agitated as a sparrow at the mercy of a hawk.

When his hooded eyes swung in her direction she saw him smile; the sight struck her as far from pleasant.

'Nonsense,' he contradicted, his voice smooth as silk. 'Though you sound too young to be able to appreciate fine old brandy, it might help to prevent you from crying.'

Startled by his keen perception, Angie fought hard for control while she watched him pouring a drink, holding the glass with one finger crooked just over the edge, using the tip to warn him not to over-pour. She sensed his satisfaction when he set that glass aside for himself, then picked up another one which he filled to the same level, but this time without the aid of a finger gauge.

'Have I managed to pour the same quantity in each?' he asked, holding up both glasses for her inspection.

She nodded, bemused, then reminded that he could not see, stammered, 'Yes . . .'

'Good!' Her heart almost stopped beating when he grinned. 'It is becoming easier to judge by the sound, whether I have poured enough, and by the relative weight of decanter and glass.'

Though it was becoming easier by the minute to understand Cilla's fear of the dominating Greek, as she took the proffered glass Angie could not help but admire the tenacity of the man who was determined to stride without fear through his world of darkness.

'Tell me about Priscilla's new fiancé,' he drawled.

The request was so startling she jerked, spilling brandy into her lap.

'No doubt,' his voice developed a sneer, 'as well as being rich—and sighted—he is also very well connected?'

She drew in a deep breath. 'Well, yes, as a matter of fact he is, but I'm certain that David Montgomery's circumstances played no part in influencing my sister's choice.'

'And I am equally certain that they did.' He leant forward so that she could see a muscle twitching in his cheek.

'Cilla's not like that,' she began, 'she——'

'All women are like *that*!' he jeered hatefully. 'Wealth is to woman what pearls are to oysters—greatly coveted, painfully nurtured, and once possessed so tightly secreted that only death can prise them apart.'

'You seem to have developed a very low opinion of the girl you once claimed to love,' she husked, shaken by his depth of cynicism.

'And who claimed to love *me*,' he reminded her harshly, 'haven't I the right to feel disillusioned when the woman who professed herself eager to love, honour and obey could not wait even until I had been discharged from hospital before writing to inform me that so far as she was concerned the fact that I had lost my sight relieved her of all obligations? I had to comfort the nurse who read out that letter,' he told her simply. 'She was so upset that I was accused by her superior of making her cry.'

'Oh, no!' Angie's shame was agonising. 'I didn't know—believe me, I'm terribly sorry!'

'Pity again, Miss Rose?' Once again he reverted to mockery. 'Are you as emotionally unstable as your sister whose love proved to be light as a butterfly who spreads her wings and flies at the sight of human ties?'

'No, I'm not!' she refuted fiercely, rubbing tears of shame from her eyes.

'Then prove it!' he challenged softly. 'The greatest drawback of blindness is boredom. I cannot watch the scenery, lose myself in a book, nor even write a letter. I'm not lonely here, just very much alone. Every letter I receive is meaningless to me as mostly they are written in English and although Nikos speaks the language well he cannot decipher the written word. If you really are different in nature from your sister, if you genuinely wish to make amends for her duplicity, then stay here on Karios and be the eyes with which I see, the hands with which I write.'

When he rose to his feet and pressed a bell to summon Nikos Angie felt herself dismissed. She stumbled towards the door, too overwhelmed to speak, and halted on the threshold just long enough to heed his last command.

'Think about it, Miss Rose, and give me your decision tomorrow. If the situation I've outlined is too unconventional to appeal to the daughter of a vicar,' he drawled with incredible negligence, 'I'd even be prepared to marry you.'

CHAPTER FOUR

'Step one pace to your right, otherwise you may collide with the door Lira has unfortunately omitted to close.' The calmness of Angie's voice was contradicted by the anxiety in her eyes as she watched Terzan Helios prowl around his study with steps that were growing more confident with each passing day. But though he had familiarised himself with the position of each piece of furniture, had paced out the exact number of steps needed to reach the door, the window, or his desk, it was the small, unexpected things that jarred upon his nerves, his joints, and his temper—a misplaced ornament, the curled-up edge of a rug, or, as in this instance, a door left thoughtlessly ajar.

'Damn the girl!' Predictably, he expressed no words of thanks but vented his aggravation upon the absent maid. 'As she cannot be trusted to follow instructions, kindly inform Nikos that so far as she is concerned this room is to be considered out of bounds.'

'Very well,' Angie replied steadily, having already discovered that to argue was to present him with a heaven-sent excuse to vent his frustration upon her vulnerable head. Thankful for the fact that he had no way of knowing how sensitively she reacted to his savage outbursts, she

smudged a tear from the writing pad on her knee
and tightened trembling fingers around her pencil.
'I'll tell him after you've finished dictating this
letter.'

'Leave it!' Irritably he strode across to the
window. 'I'm not in the mood for work today. Tell
me,' his casual tone rang false, 'is my imagination
playing tricks, or has the storm really lessened?'

Her heart responded with a leap of hope, but
her voice betrayed no clue to her feelings when she
joined him at the window to study the leaden
clouds, lashing rain, and frenzied, storm-tossed sea
which for the past week had kept her a prisoner on
his island.

'The sky does seem lighter on the far horizon,'
she agreed. 'Shall I turn on the radio to find out if
the weather forecast is good?'

'Good for you, or for me?' he questioned, his
jawline tight. 'Don't imagine, Angelina, that I am
unaware that you are trembling next to me like a
caged sparrow sensing an opportunity to escape
its trap. I sympathise with your eagerness to fly
away, for though the bars of my prison may be
invisible their hold is more effective than steel.'

She had to fight against the strong current of
compassion that threatened to sweep her into his
clutches, had to harden her heart by clinging to the
suspicion that the devious Greek was deliberately
playing upon her feelings, determined to keep her
on Karios in order to retain the services which
during the past week he had found so useful.

Once he had discovered her skills in the twin

arts of shorthand and typing he had exploited
them to the uttermost, ploughing through the piles
of business correspondence left unopened since his
accident, working her steadily for eight, sometimes
ten hours a day, so that each night she had crept
into bed feeling physically and mentally exhausted.

'My father needs me,' she told him simply,
making no pretence of misunderstanding his
motive, 'my first responsibility lies with him.'

'Does it indeed?' He swung round to tower
grimly above her head. 'Your father is a man of
the cloth, I believe—in which case one would imagine him to be all in favour of a sinner making
reparation.'

'I'm not Cilla's keeper,' she gasped, 'you can't
hold me responsible for her misdeeds!'

'A convenient excuse,' his lip curled upwards
into a sneer. 'We Greeks look upon the family as a
complete unit, if one of its members is kicked all
will limp, and conversely, if one should offend
against society the rest feel compelled to share his
burden of guilt. Your sister was honest enough to
recognise her own inadequacies. Knowing herself
to be incapable of sharing her life with a blind
man she sent you in her place—a substitute fiancée
who seems determined to ensure that I am jilted
twice!'

'That's most unfair!' The protest was snatched
from her lips. 'I've already explained that when I
agreed to act as Cilla's messenger I had no idea of
the true circumstances. I'm sorry, terribly sorry
about your ... accident,' she choked, 'and I des-

perately want to help, but I can't stay here indefinitely, my father depends upon my help.'

'I need you more than he does!' The admission was startling, jerked as it was from lips set hard with pride. 'In just one week I have come to depend upon your sight, upon your ability to sense my needs— sometimes before I am aware of them myself. But perhaps I have not offered sufficient inducement,' he almost snarled. 'If it is money you want then name your price, whatever sum you mention will be met.'

Angie winced as if from a blow. 'No amount of money could compensate for having to live with your insults,' she whispered. 'Money breeds position; money breeds success, but in your case at least, money has not bred breeding!'

As punishment for her temerity, Terzan resumed work, dictating letters with a speed and ferocity that left her gasping. During the week she had acted as his secretary, she had gained surprising insight into the life of the man whose business encompassed a bewildering range of interests, the man who, Nikos had proudly informed her, had been born and raised on this small island, who had left its shores as a penniless orphan and returned years later as its sole owner.

'He has the touch of Midas,' Nikos had boasted, 'he shares the gift of the legendary king who requested of the gods that everything he touched might be turned to gold!'

That this was no idle boast was confirmed by letters stamped with headings so imposing they spoke for themselves: the Helios Shipping Company; Helios Agricultural Chemicals; Helios Textile Industry; Helios Petroleum Products and the slightly frivolous Helios Discotheque, Ltd.—each company carrying as its trademark the figure of Helios, the Greek sun god from whom he took his name.

From accounts and various official letters Angie gleaned that he held a private pilot's licence for both plane and helicopter and had been used to flying himself from country to country in his own jet plane; that his enthusiasm for fast cars had involved him in races on most of the world's big tracks; that he was the owner of a chateau in France, an apartment in Athens, a chalet in Klosters which he occupied only during the skiing season; that he had recently disposed of his yacht for a mind-boggling sum and had purchased in its place a powerful motorboat. It also became obvious, as she sifted through accounts dispatched from famous jewellers, that in the past he had devoted much time and effort to the art of pleasing beautiful women, distributing gifts ranging from costly objets d'art to small diamond pins with an extravagance she found shocking.

An unconscious gasp must have betrayed her sentiments. His lips twitched slightly, then he drawled, showing acute perception:

'I like women. I enjoy seeing their eyes light up when I give them expensive presents—or rather I did,' he clamped, remembrance erasing all trace of amusement from his expression.

It was almost midday by the time Angie opened the last of his correspondence. She read the last letter aloud, then waited, her fingers cramped around a pencil, for him to dictate a reply. When he had finished she rose to her feet with a sigh of relief, just as Nikos appeared to tell them that lunch was ready.

'Not now!' his master snapped. 'We are far too busy. I'll let you know when I wish to eat.'

Nikos hesitated, his eyes upon Angie's waxen face. It was not often he dared to contradict his master, who had grown more and more irascible since his accident, but Angie's evident exhaustion moved him to protest.

'But what of the little *Anghlika* who droops like a slender flower beneath a weight of weariness?'

Laughter grated from an aggravated throat. 'Despite your poetic protest, susceptible old Greek, I have become well enough acquainted with the little *Anghlika*, as you call her, to know that she is as tough as the proverbial old boot. Now leave us, if you please,' his voice sharpened, 'and see to it that there are no further interruptions.'

Casting Angie a look that communicated both despair and sorrow, Nikos withdrew and closed the door gently behind him.

'Has he gone?' he snapped.

'Yes,' she gulped. Then, made brave by gnawing hunger, she reminded him, 'The backlog of letters has been cleared, so couldn't we——'

'No, we could not,' he anticipated, determined

to exploit to the limit her willingness to treat his work as a penance. 'Now that all pressing business correspondence has been dealt with, I wish to concentrate my attention upon personal letters.'

To her dismay he took from a drawer a bundle of pastel-coloured envelopes, each addressed in an unmistakably feminine hand.

'But I can't read your personal mail!' she stammered. 'I would feel I was intruding into your private affairs. You must ask someone else, some intimate friend!'

'If my fiancée were available I could ask her,' he sneered, 'but as she is not I must prevail upon her stand-in. Begin reading, if you please . . .!'

She shivered from the menace she felt certain was penetrating through dark, soulless lenses and accepted without further protest the letter he had withdrawn from an impatiently-ripped envelope.

'My poor darling Terzan,' she faltered, cringing with embarrassment. 'I was horrified to learn of your accident . . . let me come to Karios . . . I am prepared to devote the rest of my life to making you happy . . . life for us could be one long idyll . . . the depths of intimacy,' she stumbled, her cheeks fiery . . . 'we once shared must mean that I am best qualified to act as your loving nurse, to guide you around obstacles, to choose your clothes and help you to dress.'

Angie choked to a halt, then, after a quick glance at features frozen with distaste, she concentrated upon relaying the puerile sentiments repeated in each consecutive letter, not one of which contained an iota of constructive advice, not one glimpse of insight into the true nature of the ferociously independent Greek. *They each have their own interests at heart*, she told herself, bogged down with pity for the man encumbered with a host of superficial friends. *He must have been blind even before his accident if he couldn't recognise these self-seeking, avaricious women for what they are!*

Doggedly she waded through the pile, her numbed state of mind betrayed by a voice that gradually developed into a monotonous chant. She had progressed almost halfway through the final letter before its vitriolic content became impressed upon her mind.

'Congratulations upon the break-up of your engagement ... you have had a lucky escape. Though it would not have been politic to mention it earlier, your ex-fiancée is a notorious social climber who in the past has made no secret of her determination to marry the richest man available, and preferably one with a title ...'

Uttering a cry of disgust, Angie dropped the letter from fingers that felt scorched. 'That's the finish!' she gasped. 'I refuse to read further lies about my sister ...'

She waited with fists clenched tightly in her lap, expecting a hail of condemnation to fall upon her head, but instead was shocked at the sight of features darkened by a cloud of depression, and by the lack of fire in his voice when grimly he admitted:

'At first I was very angry with Priscilla, but I can now remember with gratitude, for it appears she is the only honest woman I have ever known.'

Understanding his depth of disillusionment, she tried to console, 'Cilla can be infuriating, but no one ever stays angry with her for long because basically she's very lovable.'

His sightless stare swivelled in her direction. 'Then your father is fortunate in being twice blessed—having one daughter who is lovable, and another who is intensely loyal to those she loves.'

She left him to partake of a solitary lunch, dismissed from his presence with a brusqueness that seemed to betray annoyance at his own momentary weakness. But as she nibbled at the light, delicious meal of sweet, orange-coloured roe of the sea urchins Nikos had gathered from the rocks that morning, garnished with a slice of lemon and accompanied by slices of Crisulla's freshly-baked brown bread, she debated in her mind the anathema of a man rich in worldly possessions but made poverty-stricken by a lack of true friends.

I am not lonely here, just very much alone,' he had claimed. Angie now realised, even if he did not, that his words had been thrown up like a fence to hide a core of solitude. Was his pride a mask behind which lurked a fear not only of physical blindness but of having to grope a solitary path through a world of stark loneliness?

'Do you drive, Miss Rose?'

The question shocked her erect. No man of his physique had the right to such a noiseless approach, she decided, irritated by the pulsating shock his voice had inflicted upon her nerves.

'Yes . . . at least, I did at home.' She swallowed hard to disperse a last morsel of bread that had lodged in her throat.

'Good. Nikos tells me that the storm has all but passed, so, reluctant though I am to be driven by a woman, I feel in need of a change of environment. Come, I will allow you to drive me around the island.'

'Oh, but——' she began a breathless protest, 'I'm used to driving on the left.'

'Left, right or centre, it makes no matter,' his teeth snapped, 'mine is the only car on the island, the only other traffic consists merely of donkey carts and the odd bicycle.'

Her relief was indescribable when, instead of the limousine she had been dreading, her eyes fell upon a Mini as the grinning Nikos threw open a garage door—sparkling coachwork, pristine interior, yet in every other respect as dearly familiar as the battered old vehicle in which she had driven around her father's parish.

When pure nervousness caused her to crash the gears she glanced sideways at her passenger and saw his lips tighten, the knuckles whitening on hands resting against a lean thigh. This faint insight into the mind of the man steeling himself to being driven into the unknown, to sit impassive when once he had driven at demoniacal speed, throwing chunks of power-driven metal around curves and bends with the cool-headed precision of one whose batteries could only be recharged with the spark of danger, impressed upon her the need to relax, to communicate her mastery over the controls.

'Proceed to the end of the drive, then turn left,' he directed. 'Continue along the coast road until you reach the village.'

As soon as she set off along the drive her confidence flooded back, so that her actions became mechanical and she was able to take in some of the beauty of fields clothed in springtime green and a sea shading from aquamarine to brilliant blue beneath a rapidly-warming sun.

She was surprised by the miles they had to cover before leaving the estate behind, and when she remarked upon the groves of orange, lemon and fig, the gnarled trunks and thrusting green of newly-awakening vines, the innumerable olive trees, he replied laconically:

'Years ago, when I worked here as a child harvesting the olives, I was convinced that the groves stretched far into infinity.'

'You used to work on the land you now own?' she enquired, wide-eyed.

Terzan nodded. 'From dawn until dusk, as long as there was an olive left to gather my mother and father, Aunt Maria and myself toiled beneath the heat of the sun with only bread and cheese as sustenance and water or, if we were fortunate, a carafe of rough wine to quench our thirst.'

'Were they happy days?' She waited intently, hoping to receive some clue to his complex nature in his reply.

'In retrospect, I suppose they were,' he told her cautiously, 'but that could be because those days are always associated in my mind with my parents.'

'Where are your parents now?'

'Both dead.' He shrugged, yet instinctively she sensed a wound still raw. 'They passed away within six months of each other, when I was ten years old. I then moved in with my widowed aunt and remained with her until I left the island in my early teens to seek fun and fortune in the outside world.'

As if guessing her intention to point out how fortunate he was to have achieved everything he had set out to do, he switched abruptly to a different subject.

'Greek ancients regarded the olive as sacred, a symbol of peace and an emblem of fertility. Even today, the islanders of Karios, who cling to their superstitions as tenaciously as they cling to a way of life that has changed little during the past century, insist that a bride must wear an olive garland or else run the risk of discovering that she is barren. *"My wife shall be as a fruitful vine,"'* he quoted softly, *'"my children like olive plants round about my table."*

'Not one particle of the olive is wasted,' he continued in a less brooding vein. 'Once the oil has been extracted the residue is boiled down for soap and the remainder is used as fertiliser. Prunings from the trees are utilised as fodder and bedding for sheep and goats; the hard timber is used for making furniture and at times even forms the structures of houses. Even withered branches are burned to provide warmth and to fuel the cooking stoves.'

Angie had the feeling when he lapsed into silence that the taciturn Greek had come as near as his frustrated nature would allow towards offering an olive branch, and as she guided the car along deserted roads she told herself that the sudden lightening of her spirits was due to the beauty all around her, to profuse orchards, the waving fields, to hills topped with windmills, to blue sea lapping tiny sandy coves tucked into the craggy coastline, and had no connection whatsoever with the tall Greek sitting loose-limbed by her side, looking at ease for the first time since her arrival, his brow unfurrowed, his mouth curved upwards as if almost tempted to smile.

'Stop when we reach the village,' he instructed, as if aware that a tumble of white cubed houses had appeared on the horizon. 'My aunt lives in the house with the dark blue shutters, I'd like you to meet her.'

The house, when she drew up outside it, was a disappointment. The outside walls were covered with flaking whitewash, and paint was peeling from the window frames and door. A wooden table reeled drunkenly against one wall and though a vine-covered pergola shaded the fore-court, the base of the vine was littered with piles of debris, the most incongruous item being an empty, bright blue plastic detergent bottle.

It did not seem possible that a cosmopolitan,

highly intelligent business man could have originated from such deprived surroundings.

They had no time to knock before the door was flung open revealing on the threshold a wrinkled-faced crone, her cheeks pitted with grime, dressed head to toe in ancient, unsavoury black. Angie stared appalled when, after addressing swift, unintelligible words to her nephew, the old woman extended a hand, palm uppermost.

Grim-faced, Terzan delved into his pocket and dropped a handful of silver coins in the direction of her grasping claw. Her cackle of delight sickened Angie to the very soul, nevertheless she was not prepared for the shock of seeing a door slammed in her companion's face, nor for the pity that speared her so sharply she had to bite her lip to force back a cry of pain at the sight of his expression of patently forced indifference.

They had progressed halfway back to the villa before he spoke.

'Somewhere along this road you will see a layby that overlooks my favourite view of the island. I've gone there often in the past whenever I've felt . . . troubled. Pull in there, will you, please, I'd like a few minutes' silence to sort out my thoughts.'

Seconds later Angie drew to a halt where the road reached the summit of golden cliffs that plunged spectacularly down, then outwards to form a circle, perfect as a wedding ring, floating on a sea of dark blue satin. When he leant back his head she guessed that behind the dark glasses his eyes were closed. Loath to intrude upon his thoughts, she stared silently at the scene below, identifying with his hurt, sharing the shame of his aunt's rejection —and puzzled by it. Finally, when she could stand the silence no longer, she whispered softly:

'Why did you go? You must have learnt from past experience that your aunt is an unfeeling woman who loves only money.'

'I hardly know myself,' he replied sombrely. 'I suppose, basically, it is because however far a man might travel he always gravitates towards the place where his roots lie deepest. I cannot expect you to understand, Miss Rose, for you are part of a loving, caring family. However far you may travel, however long you may be away, you have the assurance of knowing that you will be welcomed home. Aunt Maria is my only living relative,' he told her simply. 'I cling to her because, in spite of her drawbacks, she is all the family I possess.'

Feeling her heart was ready to burst, Angie sat silently digesting his words, knowing that to sympathise would be fatal, to betray pity would be to invite anger sudden and explosive as an Aegean storm. For a long time she wrestled with a conscience insisting that the step she was contemplating was wrong, but the events of the day had laid bare Terzan Helios's lonely soul and eventually prudence was swamped by compassion.

'If . . . if you still want me to, I'll remain here on Karios,' she told him.

'As my wife . . .?'

A quiver ran through her frame, but she

managed to keep her voice steady when she answered huskily, 'If necessary, yes . . .'

At that moment a vagrant cloud drifted across the face of the sun, which was why Angie was later able to convince herself that the sight that had frightened her was a trick of the light—that for one infinitesimal second Terzan Helios's expression had *not* been transformed by a thin satisfied smile!

CHAPTER FIVE

THERE were lots of churches on Karios, tiny white-washed buildings each with the inevitable bell tower, standing square as sugar cubes around every bend; beside each group of houses, perched high on solitary hills with only sheep, goats and the occasional shepherd to make up a congregation.

But the marriage ceremony was to take place in the church overlooking the harbour, because it was the main one, the only one large enough to accommodate every one of the islanders, who had made plain their delight at the *kirios's* choice of bride.

Since the day their betrothal had been announced the sun had shone on Karios, soaking up moisture from sodden fields, reducing streams to trickles, stirring luxuriant growth into orchards, meadows and hedgerows so that the whole island seemed overnight to have burst into flower.

For the past ten days Angie had been left very much to her own devices. Once the storm had subsided and the stretch of sea between Karios and Rhodes, its large, bustling neighbour, had become navigable, further sacks of mail had been delivered to the villa, yet much to her surprise Terzan had made no call upon her services, had seemed content to allow her plenty of free time to roam the island, to accept the islanders' mimed invitations to step inside their houses where invariably she had been offered a liqueur or a small glass plate filled with sweet preserve made of orange peel, tiny unripe bitter oranges, quince or grapes, or perhaps delicious clear honey poured over shelled walnuts or almonds, which was the Greek way of instilling sweetness into friendship.

By dallying in the middle of the main street next to a stone water trough fed by a spring, she had managed to make friends with the women and girls who gathered with pitchers and pails to collect the family's water supply, to wash the family's clothes, to chatter and exchange the latest items of gossip. Even though their conversation had, of necessity, been conducted entirely in smiles, giggles and mime, she had learnt to know and admire the hardworking islanders for their personal qualities, their warm hospitality; the pride of their men, the shy modesty of their women.

'*Parakalo*, may I help you to dress?'

When Angie turned away from the bedroom window through which, for the past hour, she had stared, quite motionless, Lira was shocked by the incomprehension reflected in dazed grey eyes—the young *Anghlika* did not look at all as a bride should look on her wedding day, there was an absence of sparkle, an almost hunted look about the pale face that could have been mistaken for a mask were it not for a pink bottom lip that had a tendency to quiver.

'What? Already . . .?' Angie's eyes focused upon Lira's excited face. 'Surely it's much too soon.'

The maid's face fell. 'It is ten o'clock and the ceremony is due to take place at noon.'

'Exactly,' Angie affirmed quietly. 'It will not take me two hours to slip into a dress and comb my hair.'

Lira's eyes swivelled towards the simple white cotton dress laid out on the bed. For a reason her simple mind could not fathom, the *Anghlika* had insisted that the subject of her wedding gown was not to be mentioned in the presence of the *kirios* who, with typical male indifference to the importance of dress, had seemed to have overlooked the fact that the girl he was about to marry had arrived on the island unprepared for a whirlwind courtship, and still less for a swiftly arranged marriage. And yet, she reasoned, a mere hint of what was required would have been sufficient to have him order from Rhodes the entire contents of one of the many fabulous shops that abounded in the town, thereby averting the need for the bride to make do with a dress which, though spotless, was limp with many washings.

Then suddenly her brow cleared. But of course, how stupid of her! What did it matter to the bride what she wore to her wedding when her bridegroom could not see!

Nikos frowned when, after permission to enter followed his quick knock upon the door, he stepped inside Angie's room. Every servant in the villa, every inhabitant of the island, was in a furore of excitement, yet both the bride and bridegroom seemed surrounded by an atmosphere of gloom. Something was wrong, he could feel it in his bones. Of all the women that had passed through the *kirios*'s life—and there had been many—only this one had met with his unqualified approval. The slender, honest-eyed girl, calm of mood, gentle of voice, who had drifted like a wraith across the sea to Karios, had seemed to him to carry the antidote to the poisonous moods, the spirited temper of the man whom fate had seen fit to deprive of vision, to topple like a god from his pedestal.

Why then, as the day of the wedding crept nearer, had the *kirios* grown more and more morose? And why, now that the day had actually dawned, did his bride have the look of a lamb being led to slaughter . . .?

'The *kirios* would like to speak to you in his study as soon as is convenient,' he told Angie gravely.

'Oh, but he mustn't! It is unlucky for the bridegroom to see the bride just before the ceremony,' Lira burst out. Then, appalled by her gaffe, she clasped horrified hands to her mouth and fled the room.

'Thank you, Nikos.' The calmness of Angie's voice surprised him. 'Please tell the *kirios* that I will join him almost immediately.'

Seconds later she entered the study and found that, as usual, it was shrouded in darkness. Her heart jerked at the sight of Terzan's figure seated behind his desk, looking formal and very businesslike in a suit of sombre grey. He was twirling a silver pen between lean fingers, as she had often seen him do when he was impatient to begin dictating.

He's going to tell me to take a letter! The hysterical thought popped into her mind. A letter beginning: *To whom it may concern: From this day onward the property known as Angelina Mary Rose shall come under the complete jurisdiction of Terzan Hélios, hereinafter to be known as Helios Matrimonial Inc. . . .*

Though her movements had been quiet, he was aware of her presence. Rising to his feet, he invited politely, 'Sit down, won't you?'

She obeyed, feeling helpless as the subject of some minor company about to be taken over by a major concern.

'As you may already know,' he continued austerly, resuming his seat, 'today is the last day of Holy Week, the final week of Lent, which in Greece is traditionally one of mourning.'

Angie nodded, then remembering that he could not see, cleared her throat before replying. 'I've realised during the time I've spent on the island that the meaning of Easter to your people is as strong as, if not stronger than Christmas is to mine.'

'It is the most important feast day in the Greek religious calendar,' he nodded. 'The lead-up to this spring festival is taken very seriously. First of all we have a carnival period, a month-long celebration that lasts until the beginning of Lent, which is a time of rigorous self-denial. During the final week of Lent, Holy Week, music, singing, and all other kinds of entertainment are banned, the only permissible activities being house-cleaning, white-washing, sweeping, and generally preparing for Easter. Two days ago the islanders began baking the traditional Easter buns and dying the red eggs that are an integral part of the Easter celebrations. Easter Saturday is the day when the gloom begins to lift, which is why I was able to make special arrangements for our wedding to take place today.'

What response is he expecting of me? Angie wondered wildly. Am I supposed to jump with joy and shout hurray when for the past days I've been plagued by the suspicion that once more I've been manipulated, this time by a man who is a past master at getting his own way!

'After having been granted such a great concession, however,' he continued to enlighten her, 'I felt I had to bow to the islanders' wishes that the feasting should not commence until after midnight, which time represents to them the demise of the old year and the dawning of the new.'

'I don't mind in the least,' she told him stiffly. 'In fact, I feel it's hypocritical to have a wedding feast of any kind when we have nothing to celebrate. Our marriage is simply a business proposition, made necessary because of unique circumstances. You need a secretary and I feel I'm under an obligation to carry out that role. Marriage offered the solution to two problems,' she concluded with a tinge of bitterness, 'its vows bind me to you far tighter than any contract of employment, and the fact that I bear your name will act as a sop to your islanders' strong sense of propriety.'

'You speak as if you consider that the contract had been drawn entirely in my favour?' The silken accusation was threaded with steel. 'You make no mention of the benefits that accrue to you, the benefits of position, security, and a not inconsiderable fortune.'

He could not have missed her sharply-indrawn breath, the rustle of her skirt as pride drove her to her feet.

'It seems to me that one of the main drawbacks of wealth is the fear of losing it,' she told him quietly. 'I would much prefer to remain as I am—poor yet seldom unhappy.'

The dignity of her stance must have been communicated to him. His lips curled upwards in a derisory smile, then he made plain his disbelief, confirmed that he had placed her in the same category as the host of women who had written offering their services in exchange for the benefits he had just outlined, by mocking coldly:

'You surprise me, Miss Rose—I had imagined that every little caterpillar yearned to be a butterfly.'

It would have been so easy for her to have lost her temper, to have stormed out of the study, away from the island for ever. Terzan was using his blindness as an excuse for giving rein to the nasty impulses that everyone possessed but which most people made an effort to suppress—sarcasm, ill-temper, aggressiveness, were not symptomatic of blindness but were basic traits which since his affliction had been allowed to become exaggerated.

As she stumbled back to her bedroom only one thought stopped her from throwing her few possessions into a suitcase and demanding to be transported from the island—to be blinded by tears was bad enough; what must it be like to have to grope forever through an impenetrable, black-velvet world?

She just had time to repair the damage done by her spurt of tears before Lira erupted into the room. Obviously bursting with excitement, she half-bobbed a curtsey before urging:

'Crisulla has just finished arranging the bridal suite, you must come and see the *sperveri,* it looks *splendid*!' she sighed, clasping her hands together in an excess of fervour.

'Bridal suite . . .?' Angie repeated stupidly, flicking a glance around her room and finding it reassuringly familiar. '*Sperveri*—what's that, for heaven's sake?'

It caught her eye immediately she stepped inside a room dominated by a huge bed completely shrouded by a silk curtain, its hem gathered into a ringed support suspended from the ceiling, its pleats cascading outwards so that the occupants of the bed would be screened by folds of shimmering, hand-embroidered silk.

'It is the bridal curtain!' Eagerly Lira pulled her forward. 'Every Greek bride has one, usually they are handed down from generation to generation, but as you are foreign, and the *kirios* has no family to speak of, the women of the island decided upon this as their wedding present. Every hour of the day and night since the announcement of your betrothal they have worked in shifts so that it could be finished in time. See,' she urged Angie's leaden feet forward as a smiling Crisulla drew the curtain aside, 'even your pillowcase has been embroidered and edged with lace!'

Angie stood stricken, absolutely bereft of words. It had simply never occurred to her that she would be expected to share a room with her boss-husband. Granted, the bedroom was en suite, with an adjoining sitting-room, bathroom, and dressing-room behind connecting doors, but the spare bed she had glimpsed while on a wandering tour of the villa was by no means long enough to accommodate Terzan's length and she could not imagine the fiery-tempered Greek suffering nightly cramp without complaint.

Interpreting her stunned silence as a fitting tribute to the islanders' beautifully-worked gift, the two women smiled broadly. Then Crisulla bit out a sharp exclamation, her eyes pinpointing upon a small clock.

'Ohi! Entheka . . .!' she shrieked, throwing her hands up in the air.

'It is eleven o' clock,' Lira hastily interpreted. 'We must hurry, for there is still a great deal to be done.'

Angie wanted to argue that so far as she was

concerned ten minutes would suffice to allow her to bath, slip into her dress, and flick a comb through her hair. But neither Crisulla nor Lira seemed prepared to listen as they whisked around her bedroom, running her bath, laying out a change of underwear, and making sure that she had everything she needed before scurrying out of the room.

She sighed, exasperated, then deciding that it would be a shame to waste the water she took a leisurely bath before reluctantly donning her wedding finery —plain, untrimmed briefs and bra, a simple slip, then finally the white cotton shirt-waister that had seen service through three summers. Luckily, her sandals were new, and as she fastened the straps around slender ankles she congratulated herself on having for once given in to extravagance by plumping for slender heels and dainty straps instead of her usual choice of serviceable flatties.

Pale silver hair curled damply around her comb as she tried to achieve a more sophisticated hairstyle, but finally she abandoned the comb in despair, defeated by short curls that had a natural tendency to riot

Five minutes later, feeling intensely strung up, she hastened across the room to answer a knock upon the door. When she opened it she saw Nikos standing on the threshold, his usually impassive expression replaced by one that looked remarkably like indignation.

'The *kirios* wonders if you could spare him a

minute?' he croaked apologetically, sounding strangulated.

Angie was amused almost to the point of smiling. However infuriated he might be by his master's demands, Nikos seldom betrayed outrage.

'Of course,' she soothed lightly, wondering what fresh crime the *kirios* had committed—or was about to commit. 'I'll come immediately.'

She stepped inside Terzan's study and found him exactly where she had left him, seated behind his desk twirling a pen through impatient fingers.

'You've come! Good, that old fool Nikos was getting on my nerves, threatening an apoplectic fit simply because I want your help with a job that has cropped up. I told him you would not mind.'

'Quite right,' she tilted, still unaccountably agitated by the memory of the *sperveri* and all it implied, 'but shouldn't you try looking at the situation from Nikos's point of view? Unlike yourself, he possesses his full quota of Greek romanticism— he, together with the rest of the islanders, is convinced that in,' she glanced down at her watch, 'approximately fifteen minutes he will be witnessing the tying of a love knot, the uniting of two people in love. He is not to know,' she finished coolly, 'that what he will actually be witnessing is the merging of a typewriter with a dictating machine.'

During the pause that followed she wilted beneath the scrutiny of dark, blank lenses.

'Are you being sarcastic, Miss Rose?' Terzan finally clenched.

'No, not at all,' she blushed, unused to telling untruths.

'Then let us get on,' he continued tersely. 'A short while ago I received an urgent business enquiry transmitted by wireless, that needs a written reply. A man is standing by ready to take the letter across to Rhodes by motorboat, therefore you can appreciate the need for haste if we are to get the letter despatched before the damned silly charade begins.'

The term he had used had supplied no hint of the ceremony that erupted the moment they emerged from his study. Everyone of his servants was lined up in the hallway, the women and girls dressed in traditional fashion with brightly-coloured, full-skirted costumes under hand-embroidered aprons and strings of gay, bright beads, and the men in baggy trousers gathered into the tops of knee-length boots, embroidered waistcoats over colourful shirts, gay neckerchiefs, and soft pillbox hats perched jauntily on one side of each head.

Terzan's response to their hail of welcome was a curse muttered beneath his breath, yet when a broadly-smiling Nikos approached with a tray holding a glass of wine, a ring-shaped cake and a silver spoon, he managed with a show of good grace to drink the wine, drop some coins into his empty glass, then swallow a morsel of the cake that had been cut in half with symbolic precision.

Crusilla then moved forward to present Angie with an olive garland to ensure that she was blessed with fertility, and a sprig of sweet basil for luck, before miming the instruction to transfer some of the remaining half of the cake to her mouth with the spoon.

With good-humoured tolerance Angie obeyed, playing her part in what was obviously a time-honoured marriage ritual designed to encourage happiness and many children. Then as broad grins and an air of expectancy warned her of worse to come she tensed, and had her suspicion confirmed when reluctantly Terzan turned sideways towards her, his hands searching, then digging into the soft flesh of her shoulders.

Even before his dark head began to lower she guessed his intention. Instinctively, her only thought to save him from embarrassment, she homed her mouth directly on to his. The touch of his lips was as cooling as a douche of spring water, yet heady as full-bodied wine. For the benefit of their audience he allowed his lips to linger, pro-longing the kiss until her senses reeled against the impact of a sweet, confusing agony.

It was then, with his hands holding her fast, with pulses pounding and the beat of her heart drumming like the noise of a thousand flapping wings in her ears, that she stopped pretending—faced up to the fact that, in spite of his tyrannical ways, his searing wit and biting tongue, in spite of the fact that he seemed almost to dislike her, she had fallen in love with the autocratic master of Karios . . .

CHAPTER SIX

So far as Angie was concerned the marriage ceremony passed in a meaningless blur. Afterwards,
when she strove to remember, only isolated inci-
dents were projected jerkily as picture slides upon
the blankness of her mind) being driven from the
village in a gaily beribboned donkey cart with the
iron-jawed Greek by her side; the banter of a procession of servants following behind; the roar of
welcome from islanders crowded in the *plaka* in
front of the church; the interior of the church
itself, filled with solemnity, its gloom—so beloved, yet so contradictory to the nature of the
sun-loving Greeks—pierced by flame from tall
candles flickering fitfully over dark panelled walls,
rows of carved wooden pews, and icons and pic-
tures left shrouded in purple cloth because although Easter was due to begin at midnight, today
was still a day of mourning.

Only the tall, bearded bishop dressed entirely in
black made a lasting impression upon her mind
when, after a series of unintelligible words and
prompted responses, he raised his hands to bless
the ring sliding cold as a manacle upon her
finger—the broad gold band that acted as a stamp
of possession, telling the world that she was now
part of the assets of the Helios business empire.

She carried out her first duty as a wife by piloting her husband back along the aisle, outside the church, and into the crowded *plaka,* guiding him with words alone, making no effort to touch him or to remove obstacles from his path, bolstering his confidence with clear directions murmured in a soft undertone.

As Terzan moved, seemingly at ease, through the throng of excited well-wishers, only Angie was aware of the tremendous effort being expended by the man who, since his accident, had shunned the company of all but servants. Only she, with her deep well of compassion, came anywhere near to guessing the strain involved in stepping blindly forward, keeping a smile pinned to his lips, while dozens of unseen hands patted him on the shoulder, pumped his arm, while dozens of pairs of disembodied lips swooped through his darkness to plant congratulatory kisses upon his cheek.

Conscious of his desperate need, his complete dependence upon her ability to see him through his nightmare, she stuck firmly to his side, smiling and somehow managing to look completely relaxed as, with his hand resting lightly upon her shoulder, she progressed gradually towards the cart where a broadly grinning Nikos was waiting to drive them back to the villa.

'Not long now,' she soothed in a calm undertone. 'Take two more paces forward and you'll find the cart directly in front of you.'

She could have cheered when, in response to her directions, Terzan positioned himself in front of the steps at the side of the cart, but instead she warned off Nikos with a shake of her head, then followed up with the further instruction:

'If you lift up your foot you'll feel the first of two steps, once you've negotiated those the bench seat of the cart will be to your immediate right.'

Nikos' eyes swivelled from her, then back to his master, watching with pride and admiration the apparent ease with which he negotiated the obstacles she had stroked with a few clear words upon the canvas of his mind.

'Bless you, little *Anghlika*,' he mouthed, struggling to express gratitude through a throat tight with emotion, 'I prayed to God for help for the *kirios*, and I have only just realized that you are his response—his gentle messenger.'

'Nonsense, Nikos!' Though deeply touched, she had to sound prosaic or else burst into tears. 'I fear the solemnity of the occasion has made you melancholy.' A smile softened the severity of her words, yet did not detract the urgency from her whisper. 'Hurry up and get us out of here, before the *kirios*'s patience erupts.'

Not a moment too soon, Nikos set the cart bumping out of the mosaiced square and on to the road leading towards the villa.

'What were you two whispering about?' Her husband's profile looked knifed-etched when he snapped the question.

'I ... I was merely asking Nikos to hurry,' she stammered, feeling caught out in some misdeed. 'It was obvious—to me, that is,' she stumbled the amendment, 'that the limit of your endurance had almost been reached.'

'Don't lie to me, Angelina.' Her nerves responded with a leap when her name fell tightly from his lips. 'I am not deaf, nor insensitive, merely blind, and to the blind the only true mirror is the honesty of someone who can see.'

'I didn't lie—would never lie to you!' Her gasped protest was a confusion of sincerity, compassion, and pride. Then to her relief, as her troubled eyes roamed his face she saw its hard contours relax, his brow unfurrow as if smoothed by a soothing hand.

'I'm almost tempted to believe that, unlike the rest of your sex, you might be capable of honesty. Would you be prepared to turn that last statement into a promise?' he queried lightly, yet alert.

'You may write it into a contract, if you wish,' she returned, illogically hurt. 'As you seem to distrust me so much, appending my signature to some form of legal document might go some way towards inspiring your trust!'

Once again his head turned so that dark, soulless lenses seemed to bore into her soul. He looked tired, with a tightness showing around his mouth indicative of strain which could have accounted for the weariness of his tone when dryly he reminded her:

'I have no choice but to take you on trust. You are my wife, yet you are destined to remain a stranger because my blindness makes communication difficult and deeper relationships almost impossible. To me, you have no visual form, I cannot read your expression nor can I interpret your gestures, therefore our only method of contact is speech. You seem sincere, yet I suspect that you feel inhibited by the enormity of my affliction, with the result that you are over-anxious about your choice of words, you react with meekness to circumstances that would more than justify an explosion of temper. Priscilla would not have tolerated my moods,' the hint of regret hurt intolerably, 'she would have turned upon me and bitten, been amusingly feline, and supplied that which I miss most now that I can no longer read—the cut and thrust of argument, the opportunity to exercise my mind.'

Words would have been superfluous, so she made no attempt to reply. In a few concise sentences he had confirmed what she had always suspected, that in spite of his harsh condemnation he was still in love with Priscilla and at the same time, with a lack of diplomacy that was typical, he had made plain his contempt of her own inadequacies. In the past, he had taken his pick from a range of female companions, courting beauty when in a mood to be amused; wit and intelligence when his mind cried out for stimulus, then finally discovering in Priscilla a combination of the two. Understandably, he was now feeling frustrated by the knowledge that in future he would have no option but to settle for second best.

The climax to the whole disastrous affair was reached when they drew up outside the villa to be

met by a crowd of children who began showering
them with sweetmeats as they walked towards the
entrance.

'Crisulla is waiting on the threshold holding a
tray of glasses,' Angie warned, barely able to trust
her voice to remain steady.

'Honey and water,' Terzan explained tersely,
'the traditional welcome to the bride. Once the
glasses have been drained they are cast over the
left shoulder, usually aimed strategically at some
hard surface, because it is considered unlucky if
one should remain unbroken.'

Suddenly his thread of tolerance seemed to
snap. Without a word of explanation he left her, to
stride past the crestfallen Crisulla and become
swallowed into the interior of the villa where in
familiar surroundings he was able to make his way
unhindered to his study.

Feeling emotionally thrashed, Angie nevertheless felt bound to pander to the servants' superstitions by joining them in a glassful of syrupy liquid,
but she could not help herself from flinching from
the sound of Nikos' glass crashing upon stone,
feeling each sliver of crystal was embedded into
her heart when he bent to retrieve the pomegran-
ate his wife had placed on the threshold of the villa
and handed it to her, looking tragic as only a
Greek can look who has watched a bridegroom
kick aside the fruit placed symbolically at his feet
so that he might demonstrate his intention to
crush every last dreg of sweetness from his true
love.

Disconsolate, conscious of a need to think, yet shying from examining in depth the strange new emotion she had just recognised as love, Angie wandered into the garden and sat where she could drink in the beauty of a profusion of flowers, her eyes lingering longest upon those that reminded her of home, of the overgrown garden, the shabby, lived-in rectory, and her beloved father and Priscilla, whom Terzan had not wanted to attend their wedding.

She had been hurt by his insistence upon a swift, almost secret wedding, but now, of course, she was better able to understand his point of view. To take part in a marriage of convenience was bad enough without courting the additional burden of being watched throughout the ceremony by the woman he loved.

She glanced up at the sound of approaching footsteps and sighed at the sight of Nikos about to encroach upon her solitude. His craggy face looked anxious, as if he felt himself solely responsible for the neglected young bride. So she forced a smile and tried to look grateful when he placed the tray upon a rustic table and began with great ceremony to light a spirit stove, over which he placed a *briki*, a long-handled copper pot containing sugar, freshly-ground coffee, and a cupful of cold water which was quickly brought to the boil, removed from the flames, stirred, returned to the flames and boiled once more. With a flourish he then poured some of the bitter-sweet liquid into a tiny cup and placed it in front of her, together with the inevitable glass of cold water.

'You Greeks consider coffee to be the panacea of all ills,' Angie smiled faintly, accepting the proffered cup. 'You must find it irritating to have your national beverage labelled "Turkish".'

He shrugged. 'It is not the name but the taste that counts. It has been claimed that there are thirty-five different ways of making our coffee but only three ways of making *perfect* coffee. For you, I make the *glikos,* meaning sweet, but the *kirios* prefers *schetos*, made without any sugar at all. How is it?' he queried anxiously when she tried an experimental sip.

'Blissful!' she sighed, casting an approving glance over the rim of her cup.

His relief seemed quite disproportionate to her reply. 'I was certain it would be,' he told her simply. 'We islanders have a belief that a woman who prefers *glikos* and a man who drinks only *schetos* make a perfect combination, blending as splendidly as our favourite preserve that consists of unripe, bitter oranges made sweet and mellow by a coating of honey.'

It was easy to guess the thoughts running through his mind; he was thinking of Terzan sitting alone in his study and mentally urging her to stir a spoonful of sweet company into his cup of bitter solitude.

He straightened, well pleased with the expression on her face that was assuring him that his message had been received and would be acted upon. But first of all there was a problem she had to have resolved.

'Nikos, have you any idea why the *kirios*'s aunt did not attend the wedding?'

'That grasping old crone?' His expression of astonishment was clearly genuine. 'The *kirios* would go miles out of his way to avoid her, so why should he invite her to the wedding? He has been good to her,' he hastened to appease her look of shocked disapproval, 'far better than she deserves, considering the beatings she inflicted upon the boy when he was left in her charge.'

'Surely the fact that she accepted the responsibility of bringing him up is proof that she is not entirely devoid of kindness?' she defended weakly, feeling cold all over in spite of blazing sunshine.

'She was a drunkard even then,' he told her simply. 'To her, the boy was merely an extra source of revenue. Every drachm of the pittance he earned working in the olive groves was spent in the taverna. There were many times when, had it not been for kindly neighbours, he would surely have starved.'

After he had gone Angie remained staring blankly, oblivious to the droning of bees, to the flight of multi-coloured butterflies, to the scent rising from flowers massed around her feet, struggling to digest the unpalatable fact that Terzan Helios had used her gullibility to further his own ends, had stage-managed a scene in which he had starred as a hurt, lonely figure anxious to be reunited with his one remaining relative, acting out the lie with a conviction that had twisted her heartstrings and wrung from her so much sympathy and compassion she had been willing to do anything to ease his misery, even marry him!

She was propelled to her feet by the heat of simmering anger—he was in need of conflict, he had said; he missed the cut and thrust of Priscilla's temper! In this instance, she intended to derive great satisfaction from supplying the only need the devious Greek had implied was lacking!

Indignation lent wings to her feet as she sped towards his study, but immediately she stepped inside she sensed an atmosphere that was different. She faltered, searching the shadows of the book-lined room, heavily shuttered against the sunshine Terzan seemed to find unbearable, then stared transfixed at the figure slumped behind the desk with his head bowed, hands covering his eyes, in an attitude of utter dejection. Indignation gave way to pity as she stepped forward, her footsteps muffled by a fleece rug.

'What's wrong, are you in pain . . .?'

The gentle enquiry startled his head erect and she stood pinned by the stare of startling eyes glowing amber as a cat's in the dark, so vitally piercing it was hard to believe that they were totally devoid of vision.

As if her intrusion had caught him napping, he groped for the glasses he used as a barrier against curious eyes and breathed a curse when they did not immediately fall to hand. Angie could see them lying just out of his reach, but ignored their existence as slowly she advanced towards him, scanning with compassion traces of recently-healed scars around his eyes, the pain-creased brow, the astonishingly intact line of thick, dark lashes. Priscilla was right! The thought flashed through her mind. He *was* as handsome as sin—and as tormented . . .

It had never occurred to her that he might still be suffering pain, nor that his cloak of arrogance, his fierce bid for independence, was hiding a depth of depression which for one startling second she had been allowed to glimpse.

'Can I get you something?' She schooled her voice to sound calm and competent as she moved towards him. 'Tell me what I can do to help.'

'Where's Nikos?' Her heart jolted when a distracted hand rifled through dark hair, lending him the look of an unruly schoolboy. 'Why is that damned servant never about when he is needed? And where are my glasses—find my glasses...!'

'Why do you need Nikos?' she demanded firmly, ignoring his request. 'I'm here, I can do anything he can do.'

She almost cried out, sharing his agony, as once more he clasped his hands to his eyes and muttered hoarsely, 'There are capsules around somewhere, and a bottle of eye-drops.'

Once she knew what to look for she found them without difficulty. She shook two of the capsules into his palm and told him crisply, 'Swallow these, there's a glass of water beside your left hand, then lean back your head as far as you can so that I can put these drops into your eyes.'

Displaying surprising obedience, he followed her

instructions to keep his head motionless, blessedly unaware that as she bent to administer the drops every nerve end, every sensitive part of her, seemed to melt beneath a scorch of amber.

'There!' She stepped back, her knees buckling. 'Now stay still, keeping your eyes closed, until the drops have had time to disperse.'

'Thank you, nurse,' he mocked, his taut mouth relaxing as gradually his pain lessened. 'How fortunate it is that we are strangers. I could not bear the presence of a loved one at such times as these.'

Angie dared her voice to betray hurt, to sound anything other than matter-of-fact, when she asked him, 'Do you suffer these attacks often or just occasionally?'

'Less often than I did immediately after my accident,' he admitted, sounding wary of sharing confidences. 'In time, so the doctors tell me, they will disappear altogether, then all I'll have to contend with will be a painless void.'

'What is it like to be blind?' she whispered. 'I mean, is it totally black, or grey, or simply colourless?' she finished lamely.

To her relief, he did not take offence, although he hesitated before permitting her the privilege of a reply to the question no one else had dared to ask. 'Most days my world seems to consist of black cotton wool, but some mornings when I wake up and open my eyes I see colours and moving shapes that remain indistinguishable.' When he caught the sound of her hopeful gasp his lips twisted into a wry grimace. 'Please don't try to encourage me with false optimism. Coming to terms with blindness has been a long and painful process, and I have no intention of abandoning realism simply because an occasional scattering of images intrude upon my darkness. I have set myself a goal, and the sooner I master my disability the sooner I will be able to resume my normal place in society.'

'And when that day comes what will become of me?' Angie asked him quietly.

He looked surprised, as if it had never occurred to him that her wishes should be consulted.

'You will be amply compensated, of course,' he assured her cruelly. 'There is no room for angels amongst the living, your usefulness will end once I leave Karios resurrected,' he promised himself, 'able to live again!'

Sympathy, pity, compassion, all perished beneath his sharp thrust of words.

'You're inhuman,' she gasped, taking an appalled step backwards, 'a ruthless machine programmed to achieve a predetermined goal whatever the cost in human misery!'

'Of course I'm ruthless,' he agreed, accepting the indictment as a compliment, 'one does not rise from labourer to master of the olive groves without being so. Unlike yourself, I am also honest, honest enough to admit to my ambitions and to my determination to achieve them. I do not condemn you for using marriage as a means of ensuring a secure future; I, too, have used poverty as a spur to gaining the wealth and power I have envied in others. Do not allow a guilt-ridden conscience to sour the fruits of your success, Angelina—relax, and enjoy all the benefits accruing to the wife of a wealthy man.'

'I am not your wife,' she denied wildly. 'I don't *feel* married, I feel tricked, outmanoeuvred, an asset schemed over and won in a bizarre game of Monopoly! I refuse to stay on Karios a moment longer than necessary,' she choked, spinning on her heel to grope, blinded by humiliated tears, towards the door. 'Tomorrow I'm going home, I can't wait to leave this island for ever!'

CHAPTER SEVEN

FOR the remainder of the day Angie cowered in her room, shivering like a rabbit in a bolthole. Her anxiety had not been improved by the sight of Crisulla and Lira busily transferring all her belongings into the bridal suite, but by dint of fierce and finally almost hysterical opposition, she had managed to eject them from her bedroom—minus her few possessions.

Food would have choked her. She shuddered from the thought of sharing dinner lovingly prepared by Crisulla in honour of the bridal couple with a man scarred in body and mind, a man whose bitter childhood lessons had taught him that all women were mercenary, that their affection was never given freely but could only be bought, that cynical mistrust and ruthless determination paved the only road to success.

Behind her, the room slowly filled with darkness as she stared out of the window watching what looked like numerous fireflies flitting over the surface of a dark velvet sea, but which were in reality the lights from acetylene lamps burning on the prows of scarlet *gri-gri* boats that stole out of the harbour each evening, their lamps sparkling and bobbing in the blackness, illuminating the octopus and squid sitting on the sand and rocks of the sea bed, and the shoals of fish attracted by flame that swam into the nets.

A sound startled her, the rap of knuckles on a door panel that clapped loud as thunder through the silent room.

'Go away . . .!' The involuntary plea was jerked from cold lips. 'I don't want to speak to anyone.'

She had not considered it necessary to lock her door against the intrusion of servants who always awaited permission to enter. But this intruder had obviously no intention of being ignored. The handle was depressed, the door pushed open, and a tall shadow entered her room. Even before he spoke, the throbbing of dulled senses told her that it was Terzan.

'You'll have to guide me forward as I am unfamiliar with the geography of the room,' he told her apologetically and with a total absence of command. He looked so vulnerable, so completely dependent upon her co-operation, she had to smother an impulse to refuse.

'I'm sitting by the window,' she strove to sound calm, 'there's nothing except a few yards of space between us.'

With a confidence that betrayed implicit trust in her goodwill, he strode forward, guided by the direction from which her voice had come and by an uncanny perception which was explained when he surprised her.

'I am like a bee attracted by the scent of flowers—no perfume smells sweeter than that of a rose in an English garden. Wear it always,' he urged, pausing mere inches from where she stood, 'never change it, for to me it has become your hallmark, the scent I associate only with you.'

'As it's the only perfume I possess,' she told him stiffly, mistrusting his change of attitude, the charm that had inflicted a weakening upon her knees, 'an extravagant birthday present from my sister, I'm forced to use it sparingly and only on special occasions.'

'And what could be more special than your wedding day?' Terzan queried softly, his mouth curling into a smile so tender it held her transfixed.

'What . . . what do you want?' she said huskily, clinging grimly to the reminder that he was a devious devil and not the placatory saint he was portraying.

'I've come to apologise,' he murmured in a tone that washed ripples of weakness along her spine, 'to ask you to forgive and to try to overlook remarks prompted by frustration and pain. I try to fight the depression that occasionally descends, persistent as the fangs of a mad dog biting into my throat, and mostly I succeed. But today,' he drew a weary hand across his brow, 'the ceremony, the crowds, the noise, brought unbearable tensions that tested my strength and found it wanting. I am more sorry than I can say, Angelina Rose,' his voice dropped to a placatory whisper, 'that you were made to suffer the brunt of my frustration.'

Never in her life had Angie been able to resist an appeal to her sympathies, or to accept without reservation any apology that was tendered, but this time she hesitated, warned by an inner voice telling her to treat with caution the man who held her vulnerable heart in his keeping. Then, as she was silently debating, the sound of far-off singing drifted through the open window, a happy song of rejoicing accompanied by the music of violin, zither, mandolin and lute.

'Look out of the window and tell me what you see,' he urged softly.

As she moved forward a gasp of amazement escaped her lips. It was as if the stars themselves had tumbled from the sky and were advancing in a slow crawl up the dark incline leading from the village up to the villa.

'Everyone on the island seems intent upon paying us a visit,' she gasped, 'all of them carrying lighted torches.'

'Candles,' he corrected, stepping so close his steady heartbeat sounded in her ears like thunder. 'During the long Easter service lights inside the church are gradually extinguished until, at midnight, the church is in total darkness. Then, during a pause filled with electric excitement, the priest appears from the Holy Sanctuary bearing a lighted candle and announces to the world that Christ is risen. The church bells begin to ring out as he lights the candles of those standing nearest to him and they, in turn, pass on the flame to their neighbours while at the same time exchanging the traditional greetings and responses.

'Christos Anesti!

'Alithos anesti!

'Christ is risen! Truly he is risen!

'The islanders are coming to wish us well, jealously protecting their candles from passing breezes in order to bless our home by following the custom of tracing a cross on the lintel of the door and on the windows with candle smoke and to rekindle the small oil lamp which Crisulla will have left ready beneath the family icons. It is the beginning of a new year, Angelina, a time to forget slights, to mend quarrels, to make friends and start anew. Will you join in our customs?' Coaxing lips homed against her ear. 'Will you forgive my transgressions and accompany me downstairs to greet our guests?'

The head of the procession had almost reached the entrance to the villa by the time Angie reached a decision that tonight was to be the last she would spend on the island, so she could therefore afford to be generous.

'Very well . . .' she expelled on a shaken, reckless breath, 'for the sake of the people of Karios whom I've grown to love and respect, I will do as you ask.'

Terzan might have doubted his powers of persuasion, but his servants obviously had not, for as he led her into the grounds to exchange greetings with every man and woman, elder and infant, resident on the island her bemused eyes traced lines of coloured lights looped from the branches of trees encircling a lawn crammed with trestle tables covered with spotless white cloths upon which had been set baskets of hardboiled eggs, their shells dyed a brilliant red; piles of plates and cutlery; bottles, glasses and heaped-up platters of fresh, crusty bread.

As she stood by Terzan's side being kissed upon each cheek by every one of the islanders whose dark, dancing eyes proclaimed their intention of making merry, her spirits became uplifted by the atmosphere of intense excitement, of well-being and warm friendship exuding from their guests. The tranquil beauty of their surroundings also helped, the garden bathed in the silvery light of a full moon beaming over the top of tall cypresses and aromatic pines, fairy lights encrusting lower branches with the colour and sparkle of gems, and behind them groves of olive trees sighing and billowing down the hillside to meet the embrace of a gently heaving, star-spangled sea.

'*Yassou!*' The traditional toast ripped from dozens of throats as the islanders raised their glasses to the *kirios* and his shy young bride. A smile tugged at the corner of Terzan's mouth as, looking more relaxed than she had ever seen him, he dared her:

'We must return their toast, will you join me in drinking their health with a small glass of *ouzo*?'

Knowing it would be churlish to refuse, she accepted a glass containing a minute measure of the colourless spirit that resembled swirling white cloud when she tipped into it a generous amount of water.

He seemed aware of her grimace when she took her first experimental sip, for he laughed, a light, carefree sound that sent her startled eyes flying to his face.

'One needs to acquire a taste for our national drink,' white teeth flashed against a teak-dark tan, 'but in time you will find you'll require less and less water as the aniseed flavour becomes more acceptable and its potent effect even more so.'

'I doubt it.' In spite of her release from tension her tone remained stiffly unforgiving. 'Experience has taught me to be wary of the seemingly innocuous which, given the least drop of encouragement, becomes transformed into the direct opposite to what it first appears. In short, I have learnt the lesson that many have learnt before me—to mistrust any Greek bearing gifts!'

'Even in this instance?' Terzan's voice was rough as he slid his hand along the length of her arm groping for her fingers. The fun-loving islanders were making their way towards the tables, preparing to enjoy the feast Crisulla and her helpers had prepared for them; in a few seconds their presence would be missed, but at that moment, shrouded by the shadow of surrounding trees, they could have not been more alone on a deserted atoll.

Angie tried to pull away when she felt the cold caress of gold sliding along her finger, but she could not outmatch his determination and had to submit to the humiliation of seeing a further costly shackle nestling against her wedding ring. She could not have borne it had he forced her to wear Priscilla's diamond, or even a replica, but fortunately the ring he had chosen for her was set with a beautiful pearl, flawlessly pure, contoured perfectly as a frozen tear.

'Do you like it?' he asked sharply, his anxiety to gauge her reaction frustrated by a lengthy silence. 'It was most remiss of me to overlook the fact that you had no engagement ring.'

She told herself that she would not give in to the ache of tears stinging behind her eyes, that she would not allow him to guess how hurt she was by the gift probably chosen at random, with the help of Nikos, from the host of jewellers' catalogues littering his study, catalogues bearing the instantly-recognisable names of firms who, merely upon the receipt of a telegram, would not hesitate to fulfil any order requested by a valued customer.

'It's a very nice, but totally unnecessary gesture,' she told him, sounding prim and matter-of-fact.

'Is that all you can find to say about a perfect example of gems reputed to have been brought into being by the Queen of the Night who was so unhappy at the sight of a beautiful princess and her lover being kept apart by the gods of evil that she shed many, many tears? As her teardrops fell from the black heavens they were covered by the glow from the full moon and dropped into the sea to become pearls. Did she shed her tears in vain, Angelina Rose?' Terzan lifted her hand to his lips and much to her distress placed a light kiss on each rosy fingertip. 'I bought the ring many years ago because I was attracted by its lustre, a lustre that appears to combine the coolness of moonlight and the gentle warmth of the sun when it rises or sets. I have kept it locked away, waiting until I found a girl with qualities to match the most feminine of precious jewels, one whose skin has a soft translucence, who has none of the hard brilliance one associates with diamonds, one who is completely natural and has no need of the cutting and polishing so essential to modern-day settings. A girl, in fact, whose nature proclaims her fitting to be chosen as a symbol of purity, modesty, and love.'

The softly sincere compliment sent a rush of warmth through her frozen veins. As if sensing from her total immobility the softening, the shy uncertainty plaguing the girl standing a mere fingertip away, he removed his dark impersonal lenses and slipped them inside his pocket before reaching out to trap her in a loose yet tender embrace.

'You are my wife,' he sounded shaken, 'yet all I know of you is your voice. Will you allow me the intimacy of getting to know you better in the only way left to me—by touch?'

His caressing hand against her cheek stroked a wave of weakness through her body. 'Do you realise,' he reverted to teasing in a tone smooth as pelt, sweet as Greek honey, 'that I have no idea what height you are; whether you are rounded or slim; whether your hair is fair or dark, your skin pale as cream or rosy as a peach?' As his breath feathered lightly over lids swept down to hide raging panic from piercing amber eyes Angie was ashamed of feeling relief that he was blind, that those brilliant eyes could not unearth the secrets of a heart winging high with hope yet weighted with a burden of doubt.

When, taking her permission for granted, he placed his palms flat against her head and proceeded to travel slowly downwards, tracing the curve of cheekbones, the slope of slim shoulders, then along the length of arms hanging limp and useless by her sides, her senses rioted, then froze to the stillness of a trapped, frightened bird. Did he know, she wondered wildly, this once philandering Greek whose playmates had been chosen from the ranks of the most sophisticated and experienced women of the world, of the sensuous, moral-melting impact his hands were inflicting as they stroked the length of her thigh? Was he conscious of the havoc caused when they lingered, as his mind became momentarily sidetracked?

'You are more slender than Priscilla, yet your height is identical. Are you also similar in looks?'

For the first time ever, it hurt unbearably to have to admit. 'As a faded sepia photograph is similar to the original,' she said flatly.

The bravely-breathed admission jerked a response that was startling. Suddenly his arms tightened, pinning her so close she panicked from the ripple of muscles behind a wall of rock-hard chest. 'Why do you denigrate yourself so?' Terzan demanded in a half-vexed, half-tender growl that sent the colour of confusion soaring into her cheeks. 'I refuse to believe that a girl whose hair has the feel of frayed silk, whose skin possesses the

velvet texture and heady scent of a creamy rose
petal, whose body trembles as it moulds itself
against mine, hinting of a nature passionate as the
meltemi, the tempestuous wind that cools the heat
of our hot, dry summers, could be anything less
than perfect. *Parakalo!*' he groaned suddenly, 'take
pity on my craving—let me taste your sweetness . . .!'

He swooped upon her mouth with the precision
of a bee in search of nectar and kissed her until she
felt drained, storm-tossed in a sea of turbulent
passion. *The miracle for which she had secretly
prayed had actually come to pass*—the mood-
ridden, fiery-tempered, intolerant, enigmatic Greek
had actually fallen in love with her!

Her state of bemused happiness lasted throughout the hours that they danced to the music of
fiddle and flute, listened to songs of love made
intolerably poignant by the skill of an accompanying *bouzouki* player who plucked pleasure and pain
from the hearts of his listeners, turning lukewarm
regard into friendship and inflaming passion into
the senses of those teetering on the brink of love.

Tiredness was forgotten as they all sat down
together to break their fast. Amid an atmosphere
of riotous fun the red eggs were distributed and a
competition raged at the tables as neighbour
cracked eggs with neighbour until a winner
emerged, his tough red shell still intact. Then after
a bowl of delicious soup, the tender young lambs
which for hours had been revolved over a pit of
glowing charcoal, were carved and distributed on

piled-up platters until all had eaten their fill of succulent meat.

Angie heard Terzan's laughter ring out in response to a neighbour's quip. Her head spun round in the direction of the unusual sound, her lips parted on a gasp of surprised awe, and was pinned in the sight of amber eyes, keen as a hunter's, that seemed to blaze a path of fire across her happy face.

'You look tired, *elika*,' he mocked, shocking her by pretending he could see.

She blushed, wondering if he really thought her as sweet as Greek honey, then suffered a hot rush of scarlet when he confided intimately, 'Our guests will understand completely if we leave them now.'

Without giving her a chance to voice an objection he rose to his feet and made his intention plain.

'*Kalispera*, my friends!' he called out to the widely grinning crowd, 'or, as it is early morning, I'd better make that: *hereti*! My young bride is tired, I hope you will excuse us if we retire now.'

'*Endaksi! Endaksi!*'

The word of approval rang in their ears as, with Terzan's hand resting lightly on her shoulder, Angie led the way towards the villa, her mouth dry, cheeks aflame, her senses confused yet eager, her shyness swamped by the light-fingered caresses, soothing murmurs, snatched kisses, and golden Greek wine with which, during the past dreamlike hours, she had been bombarded.

A spasm of trembling shook her when, by word-

less consent, they walked past her door and progressed towards the bridal suite. The *sperveri* shim-
mered delicate as a spider's web in the moonlight as
she stood with head downbent in the middle of the
room, feeling once more guiltily grateful for the
blindness that prevented him from recognising her
gauche, awkward shyness.

'Don't be afraid of me, *agape mou*,' he spun her
round to face eyes shining amber as a cat's in the
darkness. 'I will be gentle, I promise you.'

His touch turned the ice in her veins into a tor-
rent of scalding emotion. 'Oh, Terzan!' she sobbed,
collapsing trusting as a child into his waiting arms,
'now that I know you love me, my only fear is the
fear of losing you! Nikos says you have the touch
of Midas—I'm a beggar in love, please teach me to
turn dross into gold . . .!'

CHAPTER EIGHT

A breeze drifting through the slightly
window teased the hem of the *sperveri*, setting the
veil of silk shimmering around Angie, so that she
felt enveloped in a swarm of beating butterflies'
wings.

Her heart responded with a flutter to a reminder
of the night before—an indentation in the pillow
next to hers, a few creases in the pristine, lace-
trimmed cover that had been crushed for a painfully short time beneath her husband's head. A
silent moan escaped her as she stirred, her numbed
body reacting with the leap of one jagged nerve to
the realisation that once more she had been used,
abused, then ruthlessly discarded.

The complexity of Terzan Helios' nature was
completely beyond her. Although she was aware
that he was possessed of a scheming, calculating
mind, that his distrust of her sex had been in-
grained in him since childhood, that his accident
had scarred not only his eyes but also his soul,
rendering him even more ruthless than before, it
still did not seem possible that he could have
stooped to such deceit in order to achieve his
aim!

She wanted to drag herself out of bed and into a
refreshing bath, but her body felt charred, as

stripped and lifeless as the small sacrificial lambs she had seen roasting on the spit the night before. Yet mere hours ago she had been brought more vibrantly alive than she had ever been in her life before. Experience no doubt accounted for Terzan's uncanny ability to soothe away her fears, so that she had melted into his arms to give without reservation all that it was in her to give. He had acted out the role of tender bridegroom with such conviction that she had been fooled completely, especially when, after the height of physical ecstasy had been reached, he had cradled her in his arms to groan against a mouth soft as crushed rose petal:

'Generous, trusting Angelina, you make me feel ashamed of all the worst in me, make me doubt my belief that there is no creature so savage as woman. At this moment,' his fingers had stroked a shaken caress against the curve of her cheek, 'I am convinced that God made the rose out of what was left when he created woman . . .'

A sob clawed at her throat as she tossed and fretted beneath the billowing curtain, tortured by the memory of lies that had dripped sweet as honey from his lips before, minutes later, the flavour of paradise had turned sour, and he had withdrawn from her loving embrace.

'*Herete*, Angel bride!' he had mocked across his shoulder as he had stalked, certain as a night prowler, towards the connecting door. 'Dream of Karios, the home I feel sure you will not be leaving—*now*!'

Greeks seldom eat breakfast, so Angie was surprised when, after she had endured a desultory bath and dragged on some clothes, Lira appeared with a tray containing a pot of coffee, a jar of honey, and some slices of crusty bread.

'The *kirios* has ordered that you are to eat up every scrap!' Lira eyed her with immense respect. 'Then you are to join him in his study where he will be waiting.'

Angie blushed, conscious of being treated with the deference due to some rare Egyptian cat.

'Thank you, Lira, I shall be glad of the coffee, but you can take the rest away.'

'Oh, but . . .' the maid began to argue.

'I'm not hungry,' Angie insisted firmly, 'so kindly do as I say.'

She had not meant to sound authoritative, pain rather than pride had added an edge to a voice which, to Lira, must have held a ring she associated with new-found dignity.

'Certainly,' she bobbed, backing away from her new mistress, 'it shall be as you wish.'

The small incident aggravated her already frayed nerves to such an extent that she found she could not drink the coffee left by the thoughtful young maid. With a sigh, she pushed her cup away, wondering how she could even begin to cope with a situation that seemed hopeless. Terzan had been quite right in his assumption—she now felt bound to stay. Cilla would not have given in to emotional blackmail but would have returned home without compunction, but she could not because her conscience would not allow her to lie to her father about the annulment of a marriage that had been consummated.

'Are you there, *elika*?' With the confidence of a cat in the dark he had found her, drawn by the scent of roses, the perfume he had asked her always to wear. He was lounging in the doorway, dressed casually in denims and a black T-shirt that hugged muscular chest and shoulders like a second skin and responded with a powerful ripple to every flexed sinew. She found herself unable to lift her eyes above the buckle of a belt clasped around a flat, athletic abdomen, unwilling to meet a bright amber gaze even though she was aware that it lacked vision.

'Of course I'm here,' she told him calmly, 'exactly as you intended me to be—don't you always get what you want?'

'Not always,' he strode forward to remind her cruelly. 'Sometimes I have to make do with second best.'

The caustic thrust brought her sense of inferiority, her feelings of inadequacy, surging to the fore. Just in time, she managed to smother the pained gasp that would have told him his arrow had landed on target, and concentrated hard upon instilling indifference into words formed on lips that felt ice-cold.

'Isn't the whole of life a compromise? We must both learn to live with the fact that we've had to forsake what is ideal for what is possible.'

When his dark head snapped erect she guessed

that it had simply never occurred to him that she, too, might have cause for regret, might have carried in her heart an image of the man she wanted to marry.

The notion seemed to displease him. 'I suppose, like most puritans, your ideal man is a reflection of your father,' he sneered, 'a mild-mannered curate, no doubt, of such saintly disposition his lack of avarice would soon have reduced you to taking in laundry!'

'Poverty has many different appearances,' she retorted lightly, refusing to become riled. 'Given a choice, I would much prefer to be rich in love and affection rather than become a member of a society made up of the most over-dressed, over-fed, and over-indulged paupers in the whole world!'

With mild interest, she studied the slow rise of colour spreading beneath his tan, then dismissed as absurd the notion that Terzan Helios was capable of feeling an emotion as human as shame when he voiced a reminder so brutally insensitive that every nerve in her body recoiled.

'You had a choice, beggar maid, and you opted for the touch of Midas—even pleaded to be taught the secret of turning dross into gold.'

It was some seconds before she was composed enough for speech and even then she could manage no more than a few bitterly-breathed words.

'I had no wish to be taught to hate,' she choked, fastening wounded eyes upon his dark, sardonic face, 'yet upon reflection I realise what a fool I was to expect to learn anything different from a man who is ignorant of kindness and consideration and a complete and utter stranger to love.'

'But not to passion, eh?' jeered the blindfolded
Greek, who, like Eros, the god of desire, had no
qualms about inflicting suffering in order to
further his aims. With one swift, feline movement
he closed the gap between them and caught her
slim shoulders between hands gripping as claws. It
would have been undignified to struggle, so she
made no attempt to escape his trap but waited
immobile for whatever blow was about to fall.

He had discarded his dark glasses, and as his
head lowered towards her she caught the glint of
flame trapped in amber eyes so vitally alert it was
incredibly hard to believe that he was unable to
see the waxen pallor of her face, the trembling of
almost bloodless lips, and the sheer terror reflected
in her wide eyes as she watched lips formed into a
tight cruel line hovering, ready to pounce upon her
defenceless mouth.

'I may have lost my sight, *elika*,' he bit savagely,
'but the rest of me is functioning perfectly—too
perfectly. Until last night I had not realised how
deprived I had allowed myself to become, how
starved of feminine comfort, but now, Angel Rose,'
the hands on her shoulders clawed her closer, 'I
feel like a beggar before a banquet, voracious of
appetite, and having no intention whatsoever of
resisting the temptation to gorge!'

He snatched her as easily as the boys of the village snatched the wild grey doves that hovered and
circled around the island they had made their

home, crushing her quivering body against his hard limbs, levering her backwards on to the bed that he knew, because of the brush of the *sperveri* against his cheek, was directly behind her. With an expertise that owed everything to familiarity with the task in hand, his hand slid upward along the length of her spine until his fingers closed around the fastener of a zip which he pulled down below her waist before pushing the straps of her simple cotton sundress away from soft, smooth shoulders. Then with a groan of longing he gathered her slim, trembling body against his heart and sought her mouth, kissing her tenderly at first, experimentally as a connoisseur sipping new wine, then drinking with enjoyment, deeper and deeper until she felt drugged with passion.

To her everlasting shame, it was a matter of seconds before devouring kisses, searching intimate caresses, and the touch of his firmly muscled body ignited the charge left kindling deep inside her and exploded a wild burst of desire, a current of ecstasy that fused them together in rapture then after an idyllic lifetime slowly receded, leaving her shaken, tossed lifeless as a wraith against a pounding chest glistening with sweat, as sensuous to her as dark brown satin.

'*Glika mou!*' he groaned hoarsely, nuzzling the sweet bare curve of her shoulder. 'Making love to you inspires in me a dash of madness! Never before have I been so strongly affected by a woman's touch, your gentle hands squeeze like a vice around my heart strings, your childish curves slip like silk through my fingers, I am seduced completely by the scent of roses, pungent as the perfumed cloud that rises above an English garden after a shower of rain. I thought last night was a mirage—which is why I *had* to return to find out . . .'

A blush of heat spread throughout Angie's body as she lay trembling in his arms, deeply ashamed of her weakness, yet too much in love to draw away. Shy of his fierce Greek possessiveness, she burrowed her head into his chest, and knew he had sensed the reason behind the childish gesture when he uttered a throaty laugh and ran his fingers down her cheek in search of her small pointed chin. Tilting it upwards until she felt devoured by blazing amber, he reminded her kindly:

'I regret I cannot see your nudity, Angel bride, but even if I could I would still be puzzled by your reluctance to reveal your lovely body. Perhaps it is because we Greeks have long pursued the cult of the nude and therefore see nothing shocking in the naked form. Adam and Eve romped naked, did they not? And one only has to see the simple un-ashamedness of small children to realise that notions of decency in regard to the covering of the human body are not inherent in men and women but must be inculcated.'

She could have argued that she found his aggressive masculinity overpowering enough when fully clothed, could have told him that in order to retain a modicum of decorum between two people who were physically attracted clothing was a restraining influence upon the impulse to spend the entire day and night making love—as he seemed intent upon doing, *as she wanted him to do*!

The brazen thought shocked her back to sanity, a clear, cold state of reasoning in which she saw herself as wanton, a willing plaything in the hands of a professional philanderer, a man who insisted upon claiming the rights of a husband, yet made no secret of the fact that he was still in love with her sister!

Self-loathing ejected her out of his arms and as far away as possible from the bridal bed and its enshrouding *sperveri*, the curtain fashioned by superstitious women as an aid to connubial bliss. Immediately Terzan sprang from the bed and followed her, a striding naked Colossus intent upon mastery.

'Don't touch me!' she flared, backing away from hands groping dangerously close. 'I must have been mad . . .!' The words jerked from her in small, stumbled gasps as she flung herself into a dressing-gown and belted it tightly, showing the incongruous attention to detail of one who has been robbed and means to ensure that it does not happen again.

But employing an uncanny instinct to define her exact whereabouts, he lunged forward and caught her by the shoulders, pinning her back against a wall.

'Mad to enjoy my lovemaking . . .?' He shook her thoroughly. 'Admit it, Angelina, you *do* enjoy it, I can tell! I could better understand your foolish prudery were we not married, legally bound——'

'With typewriter ribbon,' she interrupted swiftly, 'and sealed with a rubber stamp! I used to think that love and marriage were indivisible, but to you marriage is no more than a cold-blooded business deal, a straightforward proposition with no heart-strings attached!'

'It does not mean that, because we omitted the usual courting ritual and dispensed with all the romantic trimmings, you are any less my wife,' he drawled dangerously. 'There is no reason why your prim and proper conscience should be offended simply because you have discovered you have a husband possessed of all the qualities necessary to an expert lover.'

His conceit and overbearing arrogance were exceptional even for a Grecian god. Anger was an alien emotion to her, yet her tense, highly-strung state made it easy for her to sound withering.

'The type of woman with whom you usually associate would no doubt agree that to be attractive a man needs to be handsome, or rich, perhaps even dominating, but men who lack imagination, whose sole consideration is to satisfy their own needs, do not appeal to me. I like quietness, gentleness, and compassion—I also place an ability to laught at oneself high on my list of priorities,' she concluded quietly, 'and in that respect, I consider you're sadly lacking.'

His expression of astonishment would have struck her as comical had the atmosphere not been so highly charged, so packed with conflicting emotions. It must have been many years since the master of Karios had been subjected to such criticism. He had fought, even clawed, his way up the ladder of success, had striven with courage, daring and cold-blooded ruthlessness towards a pinnacle that had gained him respect, even adulation, throughout the hard, impersonal business world. Which was probably why her cool contempt unearthed a raw spot on his tough, insensitive hide.

'*Damn you!*' he groaned, jerking her forward into his arms. The barrier of cotton that she had wrapped around her limbs seemed to infuriate him, for with an oath he ripped it from her shoulders, then pressed his palms flat against her spine until their bodies were so close not even a whisper could have passed between them.

'Don't try to teach me manners, English schoolmarm! Men of Greece, land of the patriarchs, insist upon ruling the household and demand of their wives that they remain slaves to their husband's needs! I need you now, Angel bride, so don't fight me,' he commanded, his lips teasing her trembling mouth, 'let lovemaking be a pleasure, not a punishment.' Angie resisted with all the strength that was in her, knowing she was beaten before she began, yet urged on by an indomitable spirit and the courage of desperation.

Yet he plucked her into his arms with ease, then, keeping his mouth fastened upon hers and with the bitter taste of her tears upon his lips, he lowered her gently on to the bed.

'I hate you!' she sobbed. 'Almost as much as I hate myself . . .'

'Then please don't stop, Angel bride,' he urged in a mocking whisper, 'because I love the way you hate . . .'

CHAPTER NINE

SUNSHINE so hot flowers drooped on their stems, leaves hung limp, and colourful fish lay motionless at the bottom of the pool seemingly unable to summon sufficient effort to glide beneath the protective canopies of waterlily leaves, flooded every corner of the garden.

When Angie laughed aloud Nikos beamed, pleased with himself for having discovered a method of amusing his shy, too solemn young mistress. He continued to enlarge upon his theme as he served from a trolley the light lunch that she and the *kirios* had requested.

'Truly, there is no need for you to learn our difficult language, for we Greeks use signs and gestures far oftener than words to communicate our feelings. For instance,' he demonstrated by pushing out his lower lip and patting it with an index finger, 'no Greek would have difficulty in interpreting this gesture as meaning, "I want to talk to you". And in *this* way,' he tilted his head, thrust out his chest and placed one hand over his heart, at the same time raising the other to point a finger in her direction, 'we tell someone: "You are my friend, I love you!'

The strong vein of affection running through his voice, an affection for his young mistress that everyone on the island seemed to share, cast a frown of annoyance over Terzan's brooding face. His shoulders jerked, the irritable movement cutting sharp as a knife through the happy atmosphere.

'If you don't mind, old fool——' He tilted his head and pointed down his throat with the fingers of one hand held tightly together, gesticulating in a manner that declared plainly, even to Angie, "I want to eat!"

'Parndon . . . parndon . . .!' Nikos managed to sound apologetic while at the same time directing a conspiratorial wink towards Angie. 'I was merely trying to add an extra bit of sizzle to the steak.'

'Which is already so well seasoned it does not require the sauce of your impudence,' Terzan rebuked dourly and with a puzzling lack of humour. It's almost, Angie thought, as if he resents the rapport that's grown up between myself and Nikos.

Hastily, Nikos withdrew out of the orbit of his master's displeasure, leaving her to cope, as lately he had often elected to do, delighted by the fact that to some extent he had become superfluous because there was now one other person upon whom the *kirios* felt able to depend upon.

Suppressing a quiver of anxiety, she dipped into a bowl of salad and began doling out two portions into individual bowls. She had fallen with contented ease into the ways of the fastidious Greeks, adopting their respectful attitude towards the preparation and enjoyment of their national dishes, and especially their salads which she loved. Not for them the pile of limp greenery so often seen on the plate of an English diner, they picked according to preference from a communal bowl of crisp lettuce, thin strips of pepper, pieces of tomato no bigger than a walnut, black olives and crunchy spring onions before seasoning to taste with a dressing of lemon juice and olive oil, a pinch of salt, and several grinds of black pepper, until they arrived at a harmony of flavour as pleasing as a sweetly-tuned lyre.

Angie pushed the bowl towards him, then watched him carry out the ritual, marvelling, as she did more and more each day, at the ease with which he carried out simple, everyday tasks she knew she would find impossible to manage blindfold. When a colourful butterfly flew past her nose she gave an involuntary cry of delight.

'Look at that, Terzan, did you ever see such a glorious colour combination!'

Dismay gripped her by the throat immediately she realised her gaffe. She gasped, then swallowed hard before apologising:

'I'm sorry, that was silly of me, I quite forgot that you were blind.'

Her fingers twisted nervously in her lap as she waited to be drowned in one of the storms of sarcasm that were becoming more frequent and squally with each passing day. She dared a peep from behind lowered lashes, and was relieved to discover that he was not glowering, that his brow was clear, the line of his lips uptilted as if tempted to smile.

'Don't apologise, it proves that you are becoming a little less inhibited by my affliction and, that being so, it is not unreasonable to expect that where you lead others may follow. I have waited for months for a sign that I am becoming accepted as normal instead of being pitied and patronised, and at last it has happened! Thank you, *elika*,' his smile sent her pulse rate soaring, 'you could not have paid me a nicer compliment.'

Feeling ecstatically grateful to the colourful trespasser who had winged into their midst bringing a moment of rare harmony, Angie continued eating her lunch, but with her mind on a plane so high the taste of the food did not register. Obviously, Terzan looked upon her unthinking remark as a breakthrough. She found his reaction equally satisfying. Today their marriage was three months old, during which time she had been forced to come to terms with the fact that emotionally she was too weak to resist the advances of the demanding Greek whose touch turned her bones to water, whose kisses drew the heart from her body, whose hands stroked, caressed, and moulded her into a pliant, loving, giving creature whose only wish was to please the husband she adored—even though he discarded tenderness like a cloak the moment he left her bed. Each sunrise brought a dawn of shame, each sunset a plea for respect that was crushed into extinction by Terzan's forceful kisses, so the only recourse left to her was prayer, a prayer for guidance that she might find a way of penetrating his tough, defensive shell and unearth the cache of compassion he liked to pretend did not exist.

'Do you ride?' Abruptly he intruded into her daydream.

'Yes . . . Cilla and I shared a pony when we were children, then when we were older one of Father's parishioners made us a present of a mare that I kept almost to myself once Cilla, who became impatient of her plodding, began exercising more mettlesome mounts from our cousin's stable. Do you . . .?' she queried innocently.

'I did,' he grated, rising to his feet, 'and would like to do so again. I find idleness even more frustrating than helplessness, which is why I should like to attempt to ride, even though it means submitting myself to the indignity of a leading rein. How about it?' his lips twisted wryly. 'Are you willing to act as my nursemaid?'

'I'll help in any way I can,' she agreed quietly, 'providing you choose a decent, steady mount and agree to accept your limitations and to keep within them.'

'Have I any other option, guardian angel?' he countered dryly, yet with a hint of expectation that caused her to smile.

'Not really,' she admitted cheerfully. 'I'll find Nikos and tell him to have two horses saddled up by the time we've changed.'

Half an hour later they were each preparing to mount one of the two horses standing nuzzling noses outside the villa. Ruefully, Angie compared her ancient slacks and faded blouse with Terzan's impeccable shirt and riding breeches, her sandals with his leather knee-high boots, polished to perfection yet supple with constant use.

'*Endaksi!*' Nikos beamed approval as he stepped back after helping each of them into the saddle. Then anxiously he encouraged, 'I'm certain, *kirie,* that you will soon discover a leading rein is unnecessary. These two horses are friends, therefore if you keep to the inside, I'm sure you'll find that you can keep in company with the little *Anghlika* without difficulty.'

'I'm sure you are right,' Terzan agreed with alacrity, too much alacrity for Angie's peace of mind. 'Except in the company of a really expert horseman, a leading rein can be positively dangerous. On second thoughts, I feel I am too much of a coward to put myself at the mercy of my wife's birdboned wrists,' he grinned to soften the blow of rejection, 'so I'll follow your advice, Nikos, and handle my own reins.'

'I'm quite capable——' Angie began a heated objection.

'Keep quiet, please!' he ordered sharply as their horses began picking their way along the drive. 'What I lack in sight I must make up for by concentrating hard upon the sounds around me.'

With her heart in her mouth, she confined her speech to directions, having to tell him often at first to move over more to the left or to the right, then gradually sensing, as they travelled along the route Nikos had indicated, that he was managing to keep pace without conscious effort.

Curiously, she closed her eyes, trying to simulate

blindness, and discovered that being transported on horseback through a dense black void was comparable to the terror of jumping off the edge of a cliff, completely at the mercy of Providence, the sound of hoofbeats, the jangle of a bit, the creak of a saddle, barely audible above the pounding of her heartbeats in her ears. 'Talk to me!' Terzan commanded, momentarily relaxed and at ease in the saddle. 'I know I'm contradictory, but the sound of your voice is important, it helps me to pinpoint exactly where you are.'

'What about . . .?' she stammered, completely caught out.

'It doesn't matter in the least,' he snapped, quickly irritated. 'Tell me your girlish secrets if you like, I shan't be listening. All I want to hear is the sound of your voice, for to the blind,' he stressed impatiently, 'silence is far from golden.'

'Perhaps it might be better if I describe our surroundings as we go along,' she suggested hastily, wary of his lashing tongue. 'We're about to turn off to the left towards a steep winding road that seems to level off on to a plateau. To our right, far below us, lies the sea, and in the distance I can see a clutch of white sun-drenched houses that could almost be hanging from the side of a hill covered by orchards, I think . . .'

He nodded. 'Orange, lemon, fig, olive and grape,' he confirmed. 'The village you mentioned is the place where leather peasant boots are made, the islanders have worn them as protection against snakebites since ancient times.'

'Yes, I've noticed,' Angie affirmed eagerly.

'Actually, they're knee-high, but most of the girls seem to wear them folded down to their ankles.'

'We'll stop when we reach the village, if you like,' Terzan suggested, seeming almost on the verge of a yawn. 'In the streets and courtyards there are some very fine examples of *chochlaki*.'

Resentful of his bored tone, Angie hastened to air her knowledge before he had a chance to elaborate. 'I've already seen quite a number of church floors patterned in black and white sea pebbles. This style of pebble mosaic is typical of most of the Aegean islands, I believe?'

Her slightly huffed tone seemed to amuse him; he almost smiled as he nodded acknowledgement of her grasp of local history. But much to her regret he seemed to interpret from her words a disinclination to stop, for he made no further reference to it as they passed through the one main street just wide enough to accommodate the horses.

As they headed towards the plateau Angie felt herself beginning to wilt. She cast an envious eye over Terzan, who was wearing a hat with a brim pulled well down, almost touching the rims of the dark glasses that were essential to protect his eyes from the very same sun that had melted down the wings of Icarus. She dared not complain, for to do so would be an admission that once again she had ignored his order that she was never to stroll in the sunshine with her head uncovered. So she kept her lashes lowered in a vain attempt to forestall a headache jabbing painfully behind her eyes.

Her relief was enormous when, after crossing the plateau, the road began descending and was soon swallowed into a narrow, heavily-wooded gorge filled with green shade and scented with resin.

'We'll tether the horses and continue on foot,' Terzan decided, identifying their location by the resinous smell and the sound of running water. 'The paths through the woods are winding and the footbridges narrow.'

He slid from the saddle and waited, giving her time to hook the bridles over the branch of a tree, then surprised her with a wide, boyish grin. 'Take my hand, I know every inch of this gorge. Come, let me show it to you.'

She was glad to let him lead the way along paths slicing cool through banked-up fern, sometimes slippery underfoot, and occasionally made treacherous by the exposed roots of trees poking upwards to trip the unwary. But with the surefooted stride of one who is on familiar and well-loved territory, he managed to avoid each obstacle in their path until, with an attitude of proud achievement, he halted in a small clearing refreshed by a crystal-clear stream.

'May we sit for a while?' Angie gasped, then slumped without waiting for permission by the side of the stream to splash cool water on to her violently throbbing temples.

'What's wrong?' he rapped in a tone sharp with suspicion.

'Nothing.' She forced a trill of nervous laughter. 'Except that I'm a product of a cool English climate, unused to such heat even in high summer. Sit beside me,' she urged, trying desperately to lull his suspicions, 'and tell me why you love this place so much, why you told Nikos to direct me here?'

To her great relief his frame, towering as a Colossus, relaxed as he sank down beside her. 'I'll do better than that, I'll show you.' Her puzzlement grew when he instructed: 'Inhale deeply. Can you smell the resin? It is this same resin that attracts the Quadrina butterfly to this valley each year. When their wings are folded they are camouflaged a dark brown colour that renders them invisible when they settle on to the barks of trees or upon the rocks. But when they are in flight the full glory of their wings is exposed. Like *this* . . .!'

The clap of his hands ran pistol-sharp through the quiet woods and immediately the air came alive with the fluttering of thousands of flimsy wings a black, brown, white and orange curtain of gauze that lifted and billowed for a moment over their heads before drifting soundlessly out of sight.

Angie stared, wondering if she had imagined the glorious spectacle, the magical splendour of a host of butterflies in simultaneous flight. 'How . . . splendid,' she groped, conscious that the word was inadequate to describe a beauty that had moved her almost to tears. 'Thank you for bringing me here,' she said huskily. 'I shall treasure the memory for the rest of my life.'

'I know exactly how you feel,' he jerked, his profile tightening with a spasm of pain. 'When I last watched the butterflies I remember feeling the same sense of awe. At that time, of course,' his voice roughened, 'I had no way of knowing that I was never to see them again, that any future enjoyment would depend absolutely upon my ability to remember. Unfortunately,' he grated with a bitterness that made her shudder, 'memory, like woman, is usually unfaithful.'

'Sometimes,' a catch caught in her voice, 'it's a mercy that some memories do fade, for if they didn't we might live our lives in a state of constant bitterness and regret.' She was thinking solely of him, worried by his cynical attitude towards members of her own sex, the way his dislike and mistrust of the women he had known had eroded his character. But he jumped to the conclusion that she was speaking personally, obliquely reminding him that he had played a major role in her own unpleasant memories.

Temper reared—a stallion he was unable to tame—lending to his tone the distant arrogance of a Greek god. 'I don't see what you have to complain about,' he told her coldly, 'you came to Karios a pauper, but will leave a rich divorcee!'

Angie gasped, appalled by the cruel thrust rendered all the more painful because of the harmony that had preceded it. In a state of high agitation she jumped to her feet, then had to clutch her throbbing temples.

'How can you be so heartless?' she choked. 'You take over people as you do companies, pouncing like a vulture when they're at their weakest, calculating their worth in terms of gain to yourself, exploiting them to the uttermost and then tossing them aside immediately they outlive their usefulness. No wonder you're known throughout the business world as an asset stripper!'

Terzan rose, casting his shadow over her stricken face, and without a trace of compunction assured her coolly, 'You are the only asset I have ever found pleasure in stripping.'

Only a blind man could have remained unmoved by the rush of colour that stained her cheeks, by her trembling mouth and by the pain that leapt into wounded eyes. The only sound in the clearing was the trickle of water over a stony bed, the buzz of a nearby bee, the rapid drumming of her heartbeats as she forcibly reminded herself that his cruelty stemmed from the frustration of not being able to see, that his flash-point temper was a safety valve and that therefore his insults should be quickly forgiven. She found it amazingly difficult, however, to manage to rebuke him gently:

'You seem determined to humiliate me, Terzan, to treat me as a substitute for the fiancée who deserted you, for the aunt whose cruelty you resented, and for all those other women who tried to twist your blindness into an instrument of gain. Please try to remember that I'm your wife,' her voice developed a sudden wobble, 'and not a stand-in for Cilla.'

'Aren't you?' His cold rain of sarcasm threatened to beat her to her knees. 'Forgive me, but I thought that was exactly the reason your sister sent you here. I don't think I shall ever forgive her for that,' his voice developed a resentful snarl. 'To be blind is bad enough, but if only she had come herself I would have been spared the additional burden of despair.'

CHAPTER TEN

On their return journey they stopped to eat lunch at a *taverna,* a modest establishment with a few rough wooden tables and chairs set out beneath a vine-covered pergola in a garden overlooking the sea, but with a proprietor who fussed with delight from the moment of their arrival and food which at any other time Angie would have found superbly tempting.

But as it was, she did no more than toy with the *dzadziki* that Terzan chose as an appetiser, a chilled dip of yogourt, garlic, cucumber, oil and vinegar whipped together to make a tangy cream. A silken breeze was rustling the trees behind her, the air drew soft and warm across her shoulders, yet she shivered, feeling her skin cold and clammy.

She yearned to be back at the villa, not just because the harmony they had shared had completely disappeared, but because of a wave of nausea that made her hasten to refuse a helping of *moussaka* that Terzan enjoyed with obvious relish, and to push aside the bowl of succulent peaches and freshly gathered grapes that the proprietor tried to press upon her. Terzan said nothing, seemingly deaf to the man's efforts to coax her to eat and to her unusually terse refusals, then proved that he was not quite so indifferent as he appeared by remarking caustically:

'Heaven preserve me from a moody woman! As a sullen temperament seldom mellows with age, it is a relief to know that we are not destined to spend the rest of our lives together.'

'I'm not moody!' Angie protested weakly. 'And never in my life have I been accused of being sullen. I'm simply not hungry—I think perhaps the heat has a lot to do with my lack of appetite, it came upon us so suddenly I haven't had time to become acclimatised.'

'Are you feeling unwell?' His head lifted sharply.

'Of course not,' she lied through gritted teeth. 'I'm feeling just a little lethargic.'

'In that case,' the grating of his chair acted like a knife thrust through her temples, 'let us make back home immediately.'

Conscious of the desperate importance of hanging on to her senses, and especially anxious not to betray the trust that had allowed him to blindly follow her lead, she fought the giddiness, the nausea, the cold shivers that gradually became more frequent, and concentrated upon describing the cypresses, lemon and olive trees falling in graceful swathes towards tiny coves, and deserted beaches washed by sea glittering in the sunshine with all the colours of a peacock's tail, almost babbling in her effort to appear normal.

They stopped twice, once to pass the time of day

with a man who was leading his donkey to the olive groves, and again to accept an offering of fresh lemon juice from an old lady sitting on her porch crocheting dainty lace which she intended using as edging for a pillowcase she was making for her granddaughter's trousseau.

Angie was feeling definitely lightheaded by the time they breasted the hill and began cantering towards the villa, which was why she doubted the evidence of her eyes and had to strain to focus seaward to where a yacht was retreating towards the skyline, its occupants on deck waving an enthusiastic farewell to the girl they had obviously just deposited upon the jetty, a slim, vivacious golden-haired figure surrounded by piles of suitcases.

Her laughter must have sounded quite hysterical to his ears, her voice barely recognisable when she slid from her mount at the entrance to the villa and croaked:

'Your devil's luck has not deserted you, it seems it's sufficient for you just to voice a wish to have it immediately granted. Only a short while ago you expressed regret at Cilla's absence and now, lo and behold, she's arrived!'

The following minutes passed in a dream or, more truthfully, in a nightmare. Servants were sent scattering in every direction to prepare a room, to provide a refreshing drink, to set an extra place at the dinner table, to transport the luggage and to escort their unexpected guest up to the villa.

Angie was standing trembling by Terzan's side when Cilla erupted into the hallway. 'Darlings!' She flung her arms wide. 'How delightful to see you both looking so well. Come along, Angie,' she tilted an inviting cheek, but kept her sparkling eyes fastened upon Terzan's impassive features, 'have you no welcoming kiss for your sister?'

'Yes, of course . . .' Angie stumbled forward, trying to focus through eyes glazed with pain, then shocked everyone present by sliding in a dead faint at her sister's feet.

Perhaps it was a subconscious reluctance to face unpleasantness that prevented her from responding to Crisulla's expert nursing, to the complete rest, the icy-wet towels bound round her head, that formed the basis of the treatment for heat exhaustion that was competently diagnosed. It ought to have taken less than twenty-four hours for the treatment to work, yet almost two days had passed by the time she became aware of a hand soothing an ice cube over her brow, and before she opened her eyes to see a room dimmed by shutters and Crisulla's concerned face looming over her bed.

'Sigha . . . sigha . . .!' For once, Crisulla's eyes were devoid of a twinkle as she urged Angie to remain still. Then from behind her shoulder Lira appeared carrying a bowl of water bobbing with cubes of ice.

'Arketa . . .!' Crisulla waved it away, and with a look of relief Lira deposited it on a nearby table before returning with a gratifying smile of pleasure to the bedside.

'Thank heaven you are better!' she exclaimed. 'I don't think we shall ever recover from the fright you gave us—especially not the *kirios*, who raged demented when we explained that you had fainted from the heat. Nikos bore the brunt of his displeasure because it was he who should have noticed that you had forgotten to wear your sunhat. "What use is sight," the *kirios* lashed out in his fury, "to an idiot without brains to use it?"' She clasped her hands together in an ecstasy of wonder. 'Ah, me . . .!' she sighed, her simple peasant mind immune to undercurrents, 'how wonderful to be loved by a man such as the *kirios*.' As if reminded of an order, she spun on her heel. 'I must tell him the good news, he has missed you very much, even though he has been consoled by the presence of your sister.'

The very idea of Terzan erupting into her room was enough to revive Angie's anxiety about her appearance. Gingerly she levered herself upwards on to the pillows Crisulla rushed to place behind her head and was relieved to discover that though she felt weak her headache had completely gone.

In spite of Crisulla's objections, she insisted upon leaving her bed to stagger across to the bathroom where, with willing help, she enjoyed a tepid bath, then sat waiting, dressed in a crisp yellow nightdress and with a band of matching ribbon tied round damply-curling hair, while the housekeeper stripped off crumpled sheets and placed freshly laundered covers on her bed.

But neither Terzan nor Cilla seemed in any hurry to visit the patient. After a very light meal of toast and melon, Angie sank back against her pillows to wait, tense with anticipation, for the scolding she could expect from her husband and for Cilla's unknown reaction to the news that her ex-fiancé was now married to her sister.

Why had she come? Angie fretted away the hours guessing the answers to a score of questions. How was her father coping without help? And most important of all, how did Terzan feel about the sudden reappearance of the girl he had never ceased to love? Was he regretting his hasty marriage, or had he already consoled Cilla with the assurance that their marriage was merely one of convenience and had never been intended to last?

She dozed, worn out by abortive conjecture, then was startled awake by the unusual sound of Terzan's laughter echoing down the passageway outside. By the time he tapped lightly upon her door and ushered Cilla inside the room she was waiting, all delicacy and dignity, sitting straight in her modest nightdress against a backdrop of lace-edged pillows.

'Angie, my love!' Cilla trilled at the sight of her. 'You look more like a schoolgirl than ever!'

'You mean she looks all virginal and undiscovered?' Terzan drawled as he strode without a falter to the side of the bed.

'Gauche and naïve are the adjectives that spring most readily to mind,' Cilla corrected dryly, her

eyes darting from Angie to Terzan, who had
reached out to enclose her limp white hand in
his.

'Same thing,' he shrugged, then turned his attention upon Angie, bestowing a smile sweeter than
any she had ever encountered. 'Crisulla assures me
that you have almost completely recovered, can
you confirm her belief?'

'Yes . . .' She quivered beneath the impact of
dark lenses trained upon her face, reminded of
fierce amber flame lurking behind the blank, steel
door of a furnace. 'I'm feeling fine now. I'm sorry
to have caused such a fuss, I now realise how
stupid I was to ride in the sun for hours without
protecting my head. Lira tells me that you blamed
Nikos for my omission. Please don't,' she pleaded
earnestly, 'the fault was entirely mine—forgive
me . . .?'

He punished her by pretending to consider for a
moment, but when her fingers began to tremble
within his grasp he relented. 'It will be a long time
before I am able to look upon that old fool Nikos
with favour,' he told her dryly, 'but you, *elika*,
have a generosity of spirit that makes you easy to
forgive.'

The rare compliment startled her. Her grave
eyes widened, searching his expression for the hint
of sarcasm she had grown to expect.

Obviously Cilla, too, found his words startling,
her look was enquiring, cold as venom, when she
sauntered to his side. Angie's quick suspicion that
she was not yet aware of their marriage was con-

firmed by her sister's brittle observation.

'Either you possess built-in radar or you're blessed with the instincts of a homing pigeon, Terzan. The ease with which you located my sister's bed struck me as quite incredible—if I didn't know her better, I'd be tempted to assume that you'd trodden the same path many times before.'

Grateful for the fact that the *sperveri* had been folded away, Angie blushed scarlet and squirmed her fingers out of his grasp. It seemed that for the time being he had decided to keep their marriage a secret, and for that she was grateful, for in her weakened state she did not feel able to cope with the scandalised probing that would have been bound to ensue.

Her blush of embarrassment should have given her away completely, but Cilla had no eyes for anyone but Terzan, who had firmly recaptured her hand to raise pink fingertips to his lips. Angie knew her husband too well to be deceived, and recognised immediately the sadistic pleasure hidden in his negligent reply.

'How remiss of me!' He lifted his head to direct Cilla a cool smile. 'I must have forgotten to mention that Angelina is now my wife. Our marriage took place three months ago . . .'

Angie snatched her burning fingers from his grasp, hating herself for being so susceptible to the touch of a man whose favourite pastime was cruelty.

'Married? You and *Angie* . . .?' The look of incredulity Cilla darted at her sister was far from complimentary. Then shock dulled the brilliance of her eyes as she searched for the truth and found it written all over Angie's flushed, embarrassed face.

'I think, *agape mou*, that we should leave you to rest now.' Before she had time to take evasive action he leant across to plant a long, deliberate kiss upon her surprised mouth. 'Sleep well, *elika*,' he murmured fondly, 'then perhaps you will feel well enough to please us with your presence at dinner this evening.'

With an air of command that even Cilla did not dare to disobey, he indicated that it was time for them to leave the room, then left Angie gasping against her pillows, wondering why she found such an arrogant rogue so very easy to love.

Immediately the door closed behind them she decided that nothing would induce her to play into his hands by dining downstairs that evening, but after she had spent the rest of the day dozing fit-fully boredom drove her out of bed and into the bathroom when, after a second refreshing bath, she felt so well that she knew she would have to forsake solitude if only for the sake of sanity.

Lira came to help her to dress, but she chased her away, then prepared herself leisurely, changing her mind half a dozen times about which dress to wear before finally concluding that her choice was limited to the least disreputable—the white shirt-waister she had worn to her wedding. When she judged that it was about aperitif time, she steeled herself to go downstairs and face whatever might be in store, but just as she neared the door it was flung open and Cilla stormed into the room, beautifully coiffured, exquisitely dressed, and obviously very, very angry.

'Well?' she glared. 'What's your excuse? No doubt you have a very plausible explanation for your behaviour—a traitor usually has!'

'Traitor . . .?' Angie echoed stupidly. 'How can you call me traitor when everything I did was for your benefit?'

'Really . . .?' Cilla's eyes flashed. 'Then would you mind explaining how I'm supposed to benefit from having my fiancé stolen from me? How dare you trick Terzan into marriage when you know how much I love him—how much *he* loves me!'

'I didn't trick him,' Angie's cheeks paled to the whiteness of a magnolia blossom, 'marriage was his idea entirely.'

'Because he was desperate for companionship, no doubt,' Cilla returned bitterly, 'filled with despair because he thought I'd let him down!'

'And hadn't you?' Angie drew herself up to her full height and studied the flaws in her sister that had erupted diamond-bright. 'What about David Montgomery?' she reminded her quietly. 'I seem to recall your mentioning that you and he were on the verge of announcing your engagement?'

Cilla's glance dropped, then she shrugged and turned away. 'I discovered just in time that financially David's family was on the rocks. There seemed no point in exchanging one poverty-stricken home for another—however stately.'

'So you decided Terzan was the better bet.' Angie expelled a shaken breath, unwilling even yet to believe her sister capable of such selfishness.

'Exactly!' Without a trace of shame Cilla rounded to deliver a promise. 'And I give you fair warning, dear sister, that I intend to get him back! You may think we're on equal ground simply because Terzan can't compare me with his plain and dowdy wife, but there are many baits that can be used to trap a man besides the bait of visual attraction—and believe me, I'm familiar with each and every one of them!'

During dinner she began to demonstrate that her promise had been no idle threat. Angie's heart sank as she watched Cilla's hungry eyes devouring Terzan as he sat at the head of the table looking irresistibly attractive in a black velvet dinner jacket that slunk across his broad shoulders with the suppleness of an exotic pelt; a matching cummerbund waisting immaculately creased trousers, and a cream silk shirt with pleated front, the cuffs linked by diamonds that cast brilliant prisms each time they were caught in the beam of an overhead lamp.

'Let me help you, darling,' Cilla cooed possessively when Nikos had served his master with soup.

Both Angie and Nikos froze with horror as they watched her press a spoon into Terzan's palm, then cringed with dismay when she imposed a further outrage upon her proud Greek host by enquiring of Angie, 'Does he take salt?'

A lesser person might have rejoiced at her rival's

faux pas, but Angie's heart was too full of concern
for Terzan, who was so sensitive about his disability, so fiercely resentful of the sort of pat-
ronage Cilla had just demonstrated. Predictably,
he reacted with a clipped, chilling reminder that
almost shrivelled Angie's spirit even though she
was not the recipient.

'As I am neither deaf, witless nor dumb, would
you please extend the courtesy of addressing such
questions to me personally? I can assure you that I
am perfectly capable of indicating whether or not I
take salt! Also, were I not sufficiently proficient
with a knife and fork to eat in civilised company, I
would ask to have my food served in a bowl, all
mixed up like a dog's dinner, and eat it alone in
my room.'

In spite of the fact that Cilla's lack of insight
had confirmed Angie's doubts about her suitability
as a helpmate for Terzan, she could not help but
feel sorry for her sister, who was left floundering
in a depth of embarrassment. All sympathy fled,
however, when instead of apologising Cilla opted
for brazen impudence.

'You must try to make allowances for me, darling, if ever again I seem clumsy or over-anxious.
After all,' she allowed her voice to quiver, making
a masterly play upon his sympathies, 'love can't be
turned off like a tap, the fact that you're now married to my sister can't stop me from wanting to
help you even though I'm not sure how, even
though I'm scared of not doing enough or, conversely, of trying to do too much.'

A hush fell over the table, all eyes became fastened upon his tight features as tensely they waited for his reaction. Angie was not surprised when he responded with a smile to the charm her sister had used many times in the past to extricate herself from difficult situations.

'The blame must be partly mine, I think,' he benignly forgave her. 'I have perhaps been too preoccupied with the need to appear at ease in the company of others to realise that my companions need help even more than I do myself. To most people a blind man is something of a novelty, but blind people mix with the sighted every day. You are good for me, Priscilla,' the amused affection in his tone gave lie to every assumption Angie had made. 'Where others might squirm in silent embarrassment, I know I can rely upon you to point out the error of my ways.'

Bravely, Angie suffered Cilla's spear of triumph before dropping her eyes to her plate, knowing herself defeated yet too weak and dispirited to care. Cilla always managed to get what she wanted, and Terzan, it seemed, was to be no exception, which was why she made no attempt to compete for his attention, or to join in the conversation that ranged from the delights of Deauville to the welfare of mutual friends and did not flag once throughout the interminable dinner.

Terzan seemed almost to have forgotten her presence until, as they prepared to retire into a drawing-room where Nikos had been instructed to serve coffee, Angie tendered a quiet apology.

'Will you excuse me if I don't join you? I'm feeling rather tired, so if you don't mind, I'll go up to my room.'

'Go, by all means.' Though Cilla's glance was mocking, she took care to keep her tone pleasant. 'I'll be more than happy to keep your husband amused.'

'Don't I get a goodnight kiss?' His request was light, yet commanding, as he held out a hand in Angie's direction.

Wordlessly, she walked towards him and stood on tiptoe to press a cold kiss upon his mocking mouth.

'Goodnight, Terzan,' she whispered.

An arm whipped around her waist to hug her tenderly as a precious piece of porcelain. *'Kali-spera, elika,'* he breathed as he bent to return her salute with a long, meaningful kiss she was unable to interpret, yet which melted the ice from her veins until she felt wrapped in a warm, cosy glow.

The light in her sister's eyes aroused in Cilla a jealousy that made her waspish.

'How old friends would stare, Terzan, if you were to introduce as your wife a pious little nun! Knowing your penchant for sophisticated women of the world, how tongues would wag if ever the news got around that the bride of Helios, god of gold, walked to the altar wearing a dress that ought to have been discarded three years ago!'

CHAPTER ELEVEN

THE sea shone with a sparkle blue as Cilla's eyes. On the horizon lurked a patch of cloud, morose as the frown that had darkened Terzan's features since the moment last evening when Cilla's feline observation had registered. As Nikos steered the boat across the stretch of water dividing Karios from the large cosmopolitan island of Rhodes Angie studied her husband gravely, wondering why her sister's sneering remarks should have shocked him to the extent that he had felt impelled to shake her awake in the early hours of the morning to demand a complete inventory of her wardrobe.

Bewildered, and half dazed with sleep, she had watched him fumble his way through every drawer and cupboard, questioning, searching, exploring by touch, until he was familiar with every item of her meagre possessions.

'Do you realise,' he had hissed when finally she had managed to convince him that he had reached the end of his quest, 'that Lira is probably more materially blessed? How dare you subject me to the derision of gossiping servants—you must have known that whatever you lacked would have been provided merely upon asking?'

'But I needed nothing . . .!' Her stammered excuses had fallen upon deaf ears. 'There was nothing of importance that I lacked . . .!'

'Was our wedding of such little consequence that it did not merit the purchase of a suitable dress?' he had chastised savagely. 'Did it not strike you that in our calculating society a man's credit-worthiness can be irreparably damaged by a wife who insists upon dressing like a pauper?'

'In the business world, perhaps,' she had whispered humbly, 'but here in Karios it hardly seemed to matter.'

Irate hands had held her prisoner while thickly he had assured her, 'It matters very much to me. For the time being, whether you like it or not, you are my wife, and a man has a right to expect his wife to be a reflection of his achievements!'

As Cilla undoubtedly would have been!

Without a stirring of the senses Angie eyed the streak of a silver fin through wine-dark water, wishing she was back doing the rounds of her father's parish—the only place on earth where she felt wanted, not looked upon as a liability.

'I was intrigued by the glimpse I caught of Rhodes Town when my friends and I did a quick excursion before leaving for Karios,' Cilla told Terzan as the boat drew nearer to the island where centuries before athletes had trained for the Olympics in a stadium overlooking the capital.

'Its inhabitants swear that Rhodes is the gods' own place in the sun.' In spite of his aversion to travel, Terzan sounded in rare good humour.

'According to Greek mythology, the sun god, Helios, chose it as his bride and blessed it with light, warmth, and lush vegetation.' Angie jerked with fright when his dark profile swivelled in her direction and had the feeling that he had a message especially for her when he continued slowly, 'A similar myth recounts that Helios fell in love with the nymph, Rhodon, and named the island after her. Rhodon means rose, a flower that has grown here in profusion since earliest times, along with hibiscus, bougainvillea, jasmine, and honey-suckle.'

She blushed scarlet and was relieved when Nikos chose that moment to cut the engine and set the boat gliding to a standstill at the foot of a flight of steps leading up to a harbour dominated by towering walls, parapets and fortifications enclosing the narrow streets of an old town filled with lively *tavernas* and stately palaces, scented by the aroma of Turkish coffee, enlivened by the blare of *bouzouki* music that disturbed the peace of shady, medieval squares and lent extra mystique to the open booths, the outdoor cafés and bustling alleyways of a teeming Turkish bazaar.

A taxi was waiting to pick them up, but Angie could not tear herself away from the magnificent stone archway that allowed entry into the ancient city.

'Couldn't we——' she began a breathless plea.

'No, we could not!' To Cilla, Angie was as transparent as a pane of glass. 'We came here to shop,' she reminded her harshly, 'to turn an ugly duckling into a swan—not to delve into the musty alleyways of the past!'

Nikos was visibly sympathetic to her desire to explore the fascinating scene and in spite of his master's close proximity and acute sense of hearing, was moved to whisper in her ear:

'Don't fret, little *Anghlika*—perhaps, once your shopping has been done, there will be time for me to show you some of the sights—the place where the Colossus, the huge statue of Helios, protector of Rhodes, was reputed to straddle the entrance to the harbour, permitting ships to pass between its legs, and holding above its head a torch that shone far out across the sea. Then there are the mosques and minarets of the old town's Turkish quarter, the imposing Grand Masters' Palace, and the tranquil inner courtyards of the medieval inns.'

'Oh, yes, Nikos, I should love that!' she whispered a delighted reply. 'If you wait for me here, I promise I'll return as quickly as I can.' Casting a quick glance across her shoulder, she was reassured by the sight of Terzan seemingly engrossed in conversation with Cilla. So rashly, she assured him, 'What little shopping I have to do should not take longer than an hour. After that, I'm certain I will not be missed, the *kirios* will be perfectly content in the company of my sister.'

The capital was divided into two towns, the old and the new, and as the taxi drove away from the harbour Cilla began craning her neck, eager to assess the potential of the modern hotels and restaurants, the scores of clothing and jewellery shops, boutiques and arcades abounding in the heart of the shopping centre.

'We might be in Rome or even Paris!' she gloated with excitement. 'Just look at the shoes and the handbags—and, *Angie*, did you ever see such fabulous furs?'

Knowing the diversity of Terzan's business interests Angie ought not to have been surprised when the taxi drew up, as instructed, outside a three-storied, glass-fronted building with a gold-written sign up above proclaiming it "The House of Helios" and flanked by the now-familiar hallmark of a classical profile surrounded by a spiky halo of gold.

Cilla almost drooled with anticipation as they walked inside a ground floor boutique holding a treasure trove of high fashion shoes, handbags and leather belts, pure silk scarves, chiffon stoles and costume jewellery unusual enough to excite the interest of even the most discriminating customer. An air of bustling activity indicated that the *kirios*'s visit was not unexpected, a theory that was borne out when a tall, incredibly soignée Greek woman of indeterminate age glided across an expanse of thick pile carpet to greet him.

'Dear Terzan!' She stood on tiptoe to place a kiss on each lean cheek. 'How wonderful to see you back in circulation once again—and with a brand new wife, I believe . . .?'

Her sloe-dark eyes slewed to quiz the faces of Angie and Cilla, wondering which of them was the new mistress of Karios. Then, obviously having decided her choice, she half smiled at Cilla, but quickly masked her discomfiture when Terzan raised a hand from his side to reveal Angie's hand clasped within his.

'Thank you, Helen. I've brought my wife, Angelina, to place her in your very capable hands. She shows little interest in haute couture, nevertheless I'd like you to supply her with a complete new wardrobe that will complement the youthful simplicity which, I'm sure you will agree, is her most beguiling asset. Also, her sister Priscilla must not be left out,' he smiled and nodded in her direction, 'but as she is a lady with a mind of her own, you'll have no difficulty with her, she will arrive at her own decisions.'

But Helen seemed to have lost interest in Cilla, and was concentrating all her attention upon Angie, calculating her size, assessing her grace of movement, approving her delicate skin tones.

'Hm . . . a perfect English size eight, I would say.' She cocked an enquiring head.

'Quite perfect,' Terzan agreed, to Angie's shocked embarrassment. 'I should like to see her—to imagine her,' he corrected, 'wearing a pair of the tight-legged trousers all the girls seemed to be wearing just before I was blinded. On some they looked disastrous, but pure poetry in motion on an exquisite pair of thighs.'

Even Cilla gasped at the outrageous aplomb with which he claimed as much familiarity with his wife's shape as any sighted husband. Then to Angie's intense mortification he went on to bedevil her still further. 'Also I consider those voluminous tents that pass for evening dresses suitable only for middle-aged ladies whose hips have spread, therefore, when you are dressing my wife please bear in mind, Helen,' he flashed an impudent grin, 'that I am no dog-in-the-manger, that even though I am deprived of the pleasure myself I have no objection to other men being treated to the sight of a wasped-in waist and a delectable deep cleavage.'

With cheeks afire, Angie squeezed his fingers, mutely begging him to stop his tormenting before he should be tempted to reveal that she had a mole that could be hidden by even the briefest of bikini tops, or that there was a certain spot along her spine that she could not bear to have tickled. She knew he had read her mind when he laughed aloud, and her shyness increased when Helen and other hovering members of her staff joined in until the whole room seemed to be rollicking with merriment, milling with curious, smiling good-humoured faces. With the exception of one—Cilla's expression was set with fury, an ivory mask studded with a pair of glittering, ice-blue gems.

Most men, Angie felt certain, would have been glad to have been relieved of the boredom of deciding which clothes were most suited to their wives, but when Helen suggested that Terzan might retire to the privacy of her office to drink coffee, smoke a cigar, or listen in comfort to a programme of piped music, he declined firmly and insisted upon accompanying them to the first floor showroom where models were waiting to parade the best of the House of Helios collection.

Although he had complimented Helen on her excellent taste, once the parade began he took complete control, listening intently to Helen's detailed description of each garment, feeling the texture of the different clothes, then choosing with unerring instinct the outfits most flattering to his wife's delicate slim-boned figure. His questions were endless.

'Blue, did you say? What shade of blue exactly . . .?'

'Yes, we'll take that one, a deep mauve tint will add a haunting depth to her grey eyes.'

'White lace is very appropriate for a novice bride, don't you agree, Helen?' Terzan quipped.

'I like the rustling sound of the pale grey taffeta, but I fear my wife might find a strapless bodice too much of a threat to her modesty!'

Long before an hour had passed Angie felt forced to protest. 'Please, Terzan, there's no need for such extravagance, it will take years to wear out the items you've already bought!'

'Such dresses are not meant to be worn out, darling,' Cilla drawled, envious, yet elated by the number of outfits Terzan had earmarked for herself. 'The wives of multi-millionaires discard their wardrobes immediately the fashion scene changes, then the whole exciting replacement programme begins all over again.'

'But that's disgraceful!' Angie gasped, appalled by such shocking waste and only vaguely comforted by the thought that her position as Terzan's wife was as fickle and unstable as the fashion scene, and that she would probably never be called upon to sit through a second similar parade.

Outvoted by her husband's determination to boast the world's best-dressed wife and by Cilla's equal determination to prolong a situation that promised unique personal gain, she sank back defeated, wondering what possible use she would find, back home in her father's parish, for a gold lamé tunic with matching trousers, a multi-coloured lamé brocade that plunged alarmingly low at the back, a bewildering number of ball gowns fashioned from embroidered tulle, satin ribbons, organdie roses and clustered seed pearls, and silk day dresses and casual cottons with fluttering skirts in dragonfly colours and confetti prints.

By the time Terzan had forced her to endure a gamut of embarrassed emotions by insisting upon having an entire collection of seductive lingerie minutely described, the time of her arranged meeting with Nikos had long passed. Hoping the patient Greek might still be waiting, and convinced that there was nothing left in the entire building that had not already been put on show, she seized upon the warmth of the atmosphere as an excuse to escape.

'Terzan, I must go outside for a breath of air, it's so terribly stuffy in here.'

Much to her chagrin, Helen overheard her remark and was immediately affronted.

'I'm sorry,' she apologised stiffly, 'I had not realised that you were suffering discomfort.

Usually the girls who model our collection are quick to complain if humidity threatens to make changing difficult; I'll order the air-conditioning to be adjusted.'

'Oh, I didn't mean . . .!' Angie stammered in distress as Helen turned on her heel and disappeared behind a curtain of heavy red velvet.

'Just as well, little liar,' Terzan's mocking murmur teased the tip of one burning ear, 'that we are about to progress towards choosing furs, otherwise, caught between the chill of Helen's justifiable displeasure and a maximum draught from a highly efficient air-conditioning system, you could be in danger of frostbite.'

'I don't like furs,' she quivered truthfully.

'Even so, you must not be selfish,' he chided, then betrayed shrewd insight into Cilla's character by continuing dryly, 'Your sister would never forgive you if you should try to deprive her of any crumbs that might drop from your table.'

Nevertheless, she felt impelled to continue her fight. 'I know that you find Cilla amusing and that you much prefer her company to mine, so why——' She broke off abruptly when his head snapped erect.

In a tone that had developed an edge sharper than a knife, he commanded, 'You are to remain by my side always, is that understood? Your voice enables me to see, I rely upon your concise directions, therefore your presence is essential if I am not to be left floundering, led like a blinkered mule through the streets of the city!'

Perhaps it was her unquestioning obedience that allowed his attitude to soften as they toured a show-room lined with racks of furs. With a pang of dis-quiet, Angie noted a silver fox pelt draped along the width of a couch, giving an impression that the animal was alive and restfully sleeping. She shuddered and turned away, only to be confronted by further proof of man's cruelty to creatures of the wild, and woman's grasping determination to be pampered, envied and admired, at whatever the cost.

With a cry of delight Cilla slid her arms into sleeves of a full-length lynx coat and hugged the collar close beneath her chin as she posed and pouted at her reflection in a gilded mirror. Filled with a covetous envy that caused her to babble, she appealed to Angie:

'Isn't this simply out of this world . . .!'

'The animals that were slaughtered to provide the pelts most certainly are,' Angie responded with a tartness that caused Terzan's eyebrows to rise.

'I do believe you meant it when you said you disliked furs?' He sounded as surprised as a hunter who had stumbled upon a strange, unrecorded species.

'Dislike is too mild a word to describe the way I feel about the wholesale destruction of beautiful wild beasts for no better reason than to allow rich, over-pampered women to add to their collection of status symbols,' she croaked, repelled by the atmo-sphere of cruelty engendered by racks hung heavy with the pitiful remains of once magnificent beasts.

Finding it difficult to equate such a spate of heated indignation with her serene, usually inarticulate sister, Cilla snapped:

'How ridiculous!' Then, fearing Angie's attitude might deprive her of the fur she was hugging around her body like a woman possessed, completely in the clutches of lynx claws, she reminded her harshly, 'A great number of animals, especially mink, are bred specifically to be——'

'Murdered . . .?' Angie flashed, sickened by the implication that, because they were available in abundance, the fate of the small creatures was of little consequence.

Motivated by the best of intentions, Helen hastened to interrupt by approaching Angie with a short jacket draped over her arm, then proceeded to display complete ignorance of the depths of her client's sensitivity by inviting her to inspect the jacket fashioned from pale fawn skins, soft and supple as velvet.

'As you have an aversion to furs, perhaps this jacket will be more to your liking—it has been made up specially for a customer, but if you wish we could get one tailored exactly to your measurements?' Without waiting for a reply, she stepped closer and held out the jacket, inviting Angie to run her fingers over the limp pelt. 'As you can see, it is made of finest kid—only healthy, unmarked youngsters are culled from the herds of deer that were imported here years ago to discourage snakes, but which have multiplied so rapidly that they are now threatening to overrun our island.'

Guided by Angie's gasp of outrage, Terzan reached out to grasp her trembling fingers, but instead of offering the comfort she was expecting he confounded her by mocking sarcastically:

'Before my wife is moved to sacrifice her own tender skin in a bid to save the deer population, we had better call it a day, Helen.' He pulled Angie aside to murmur in her ear alone. 'Well, Goody Two-Shoes,' his thin lips widened when she recoiled from the knowledge that he had discussed her with Cilla, 'your feeble excuses and high-minded protests might have carried more conviction had I not overheard your whispered assignation with Nikos.' With startling suddenness his whisper turned into a hiss. 'Must you make it obvious that you prefer anyone's company to mine—even that of a servant?'

Contemptuously he flung her hand aside and spun on his heel to order, 'Take whichever coat you wish, Priscilla! You deserve to be rewarded for your honest refusal to pretend that a woman's happiness is not dependent upon the thrill of looking in shop windows and of buying all that a man can be persuaded to pay for. You at least are not too proud to allow yourself to be pampered and cherished, nor too stubborn to admit that woman is a silver dish designed to display only golden apples!'

CHAPTER TWELVE

WITH the wickedly expensive lynx coat slung over her arm, Cilla looked jubilant when they entered the foyer of the luxury hotel where a table had been booked for lunch.

'I'm sorry about this,' Terzan frowned, tightening his grip upon Angie's arm. 'Nikos must have assumed that because I have often used the facilities of this hotel for business conferences it would be a suitable place for a private lunch. I should have warned him that we would prefer to eat in less pretentious surroundings. There are some excellent *tavernas* nearby if you feel you would like to try some other place?'

'Darling,' Cilla trilled, enthralled by the expanse of marble floor, walls of smoked glass, a scattering of over-stuffed leather couches and armchairs huge futuristically designed chandeliers, and a cold chromium glitter that seemed to be everywhere 'there *is* no other place!'

Angie sensed that he was waiting for her to indicate a preference, but she kept silent, overawed by a miniature jungle of tropical plants with stems thick as a man's wrist shooting to the full height of the ceiling, and leaves that she could have wrapped around her body with yards to spare.

'Well, Angelina . . .?' As usual he sounded impatient. 'Are you happy to lunch here or not?'

'I don't mind,' she stammered, then, remembering his preference for places that were familiar, she hastened to add, 'As a table has already been reserved it would be impolite not to make use of it.'

The dining-room was crowded with elegantly-dressed people whose subdued murmurings rose above the clink of serving dishes and the tinkle of cutlery, then fell into a hush immediately Terzan was recognised. Angie felt his fingers biting into her arm and knew he was aware that he had become the subject of all eyes. Her heart panicked for the proud Greek with the courage to take on the world blindfolded, and became even more agitated when a smiling maître d'hotel quickly approached wearing a self-congratulatory smile.

'Welcome, sir,' he bowed. 'We are pleased to be honoured once again by your custom. I am pleased to be able to tell you that although we were given short notice of your visit, I have been able to reserve your usual table.'

Suddenly Angie knew she could not bear to see Terzan being put through the ordeal of negotiating a maze of tables and of progressing through a meal seated prominently in the view of every curious diner.

'Er . . . if you don't mind, I think I would prefer to sit in one of your charming side booths, they look so cosy and intimate,' she blushed a fiery red as she stumbled an awkward apology. 'I . . . I'm not used to dining in such huge establishments, I'd like to sit where I can see everything without being overlooked.'

'Angie, for heaven's sake!' Cilla drew in an exasperated breath.

'See to it, Andreas,' Terzan ordered smoothly communicating by the increased pressure of his fingers upon her arm that he had guessed the motive behind her request and was relieved and grateful for her understanding.

Blissfully oblivious to the new current of warmth flowing between her two companions, Cilla prattled happily all during the meal, casting triumphant glances at her sister, whose subdued replies and downcast lashes hid trembling awareness of a husband whose light-fingered touch was electrifying. Terzan, too, seemed preoccupied, which was probably why Cilla did not hesitate to fall in with his wishes when, as they approached the end of the meal, he suggested apologetically:

'As I am so seldom in Rhodes these days, I feel I must take advantage of this visit to attend to some urgent business. Would you mind very much, Priscilla, if we left you to your own devices for the next couple of hours?'

'We . . .?' she queried suspiciously.

Ever so slightly his nostrils flared, but his tone remained smooth as he responded to her inquisition. 'I shall need Angelina with me to take notes.

'Oh, in that case,' she shrugged, 'carry on by all means.' Suddenly her expression brightened. 'Come to think of it, I'm certain I saw a beauty salon as we passed through the hotel foyer. As I'm long overdue a professional hairdo, I might as well utilise the time by making an appointment.'

As if anxious to make amends for his absence, Terzan insisted upon arranging the appointment there and then, and gratified Cilla still further by insisting that whatever expenses she incurred were added to his account.

'You're so generous, Terzan darling,' she glowed as they prepared to take leave of her, 'but at least,' her derogatory glance flickered over Angie, 'you do gain from me the satisfaction of knowing that your kindness is fully appreciated.'

With what seemed to Angie almost indecent haste, he ushered her out of the hotel and into a waiting taxi, then surprised her still further by instructing the driver:

'To the Old Town, *parakalo!*'

'You have business in the Old Town?' she faltered, as they were sped away from office blocks built squarely in the centre of what was obviously the island's hub of business activity.

'Very important business,' he assured her solemnly, 'a pressing obligation to ensure that you do not return to Karios disappointed at having been deprived of a chance to tour the sights you are pining to see.'

'You mean you *lied* to Cilla?' she gasped, shocked by such a lack of conscience.

'Certainly I did,' he confessed promptly, 'with as little compunction as you lied to me, firstly about feeling faint and then about having an aversion to wearing animal skins.'

'I did not lie to you, Terzan,' she defended with a quiet dignity that caused him a frown. 'Since early childhood I've been taught that it's wrong to lie, and I would never do so unless forced by exceptional circumstances.'

'Such as . . .?'

'When to tell the truth would inflict even more serious damage,' she countered evenly.

'Then you are a gullible little fool just asking to be hurt,' he told her roughly, yet with an odd inflection in his voice that made her suspect that probably for the first time in his life the unscrupulous Greek was nonplussed.

In spite of an atmosphere of constraint, Angie's spirits rose when the taxi drew up in the shadow of massive grey ramparts beyond which rose the battlements of an ancient castle ringed by a belt of sombre green trees.

'The town's fortifications were built early in the fourteenth century to repel attacks from pirates and Egyptian Moslems,' he told her as they strolled through the gateway into the courtyard of a house built of solid stone with an immense coat of arms carved over a porched entrance. 'Let me test my powers of recall!' He hesitated, to run his hands along the rim of an antiquated wellhead, and frowned as he concentrated hard upon reviving memories of a scene his sighted eyes had taken too much for granted. 'To our left there should be a pyramid of cannonballs which, judging from the shouts issuing from that direction, are still being utilised as goalposts by the schoolboy population?'

'Correct,' Angie encouraged with a gurgle of laughter.

'If we continue along the narrow cobbled alleyway ahead,' he instructed, 'we will enter a square with a colourfully tiled fountain that sits like the hub of a wheel within streets full of bazaars radiating like spokes from its centre.'

It would have been impossible to explore the Old Town thoroughly in the time they had to spare, so by tacit consent they meandered hand in hand along narrow cobblestoned streets lined with medieval façades set so close together they cast a permanent shadow, making it easy to imagine scarlet-cloaked knights patrolling the silent alleyways, searching the night with dim lanterns for the presence of spies or would-be marauders.

Then, just as Terzan had indicated, they passed through an archway into a square filled with the noise and bustle of traders calling out their wares, urging milling tourists in the direction of open-fronted shops packed to bursting point with handmade lace, olivewood carvings, Turkish brass and copper pots, ceramics, leatherwork, sponges, silverware and string upon string of the worry beads that seemed an essential appendage to the peace of mind of every superstitious Greek, young or old, rich and poor alike.

'Would madame like a coffee? A cake, perhaps . . .? Please come into my kitchen and make your own choice,' a persistent tea-shop owner urged as Angie paused wide-eyed before a display of tempting confectionery.

'It will please him very much if you accept his invitation,' Terzan encouraged her with a smile. 'It is Greek practice for the customer to enter the kitchen and inspect the array of cooking utensils—even to look into the refrigerator if he should so wish.'

'That won't be necessary,' she refused hastily, embarrassed by the thought, then hesitated, bemused by an assortment of mouthwatering pastries filled with cream, chopped almonds and walnuts steeped in honey.

'*Parakalo* . . .!' When the anxious trader pleaded with her to sit down in the sign language that Nikos had demonstrated—smiling and extending his hand palm downward to pat an imaginary dog—she broke into delighted laughter.

'Terzan, may we . . .?' she gurgled. 'We needn't take too long.'

But sitting on a pleasant terrace, with the caress of the sun against their cheeks, refreshing iced coffee to hand, and the romantic *bouzouki* music mingling with passionate cries from the colourful market place spelled disaster to their timetable. At first they were content to rest in companionable silence, but when Terzan began to speak she became enraptured by words that revealed a loneliness of spirit he kept buried deep behind a façade of arrogant independence.

'I used to spend hours just sitting watching the world go by. When I was young and penniless it was my favourite pastime. After my evening meal, once the day's work was over, I would treat myself to a newspaper and look for a boulevard café with a vacant back-row seat near to a window, then, once the newspaper had been read from cover to cover, I would chat with a neighbour to pass the time away or, more often than not, just sit quietly appreciating the beauty of the girls walking by, laughing at the antics of the boys who invariably trooped behind them; listening to the endless talkers; being slightly irritated by strident laughers, always amused, very seldom bored.'

'But was he ever lonely, that young boy of long ago?' she probed softly. 'Did he ever wish for a companion to share his solitude?'

'Sometimes,' he admitted gravely, 'usually when instead of being the watcher, I felt myself becoming an object of attention. We Greeks are a gregarious race, you understand, we love crowds and are suspicious of anyone who shuns society. Also,' his teeth flashed white in a grin of self-mockery, 'we are very inquisitive, which is why in Greece you will never see houses built in solitude as they so often are in your country.'

'Yet I can't believe that you were alone from choice, not when you've demonstrated so plainly your liking for feminine company.'

'Ah, but I was poor then, and very ambitious. Girls are expensive entertainment, and every drachma I earned was being invested in ways that were to make me my fortune.'

'Not all girls are mercenary,' she had to protest. 'For some it's enough to feel loved and wanted.'

'Then tell me why it is that the world's most

beautiful women are married to the world's richest men?' he jeered, yet not unkindly. 'It is a man's nature to covet that which is most unattainable, he must always be the winner, never be content with second prize.'

'Is that all marriage means to you?' she croaked. 'Do you ask nothing more of a wife except that she should be sufficiently beautiful to be regarded as a prize? Do you consider yourself an also-ran simply because you feel deprived of cheque-book love?'

She had imagined that he could not hurt her any more than he already had, until with a casual shrug he confessed, 'There is little point in competing in a race when one cannot see the tape, and by the same token, the incentive to own a beautiful wife diminishes when one can only make love in Braille. However, though I am in no position to contradict your assertion that the face that feels to me like a perfect cameo is plain, I am beginning to suspect that whatever you may lack in looks is compensated by the sort of intelligence that is nur-/tured and developed so well in your excellent public schools, by diplomacy and tact, and by an elusive quality that no amount of money can buy, a poise and refinement that I can only define as class. It is a novelty for me to be in the company of a female who takes nothing for granted, who is never blasé or bored, who is not totally empty-headed, who does not consider a wallet full of credit cards a passport to heaven. I have yet to discover, *elika*, the sort of reward you truly appreciate. If luxury goods have no appeal, then tell me what present I can buy that will make you happy.'

'Happiness can't be bought in a shop,' Angie choked, appalled by his depth of cynicism, debased by the realisation that to him she was no more than a voice, a scent, a shy, immature body he could ignite at a whim into a flame of passion yet which mentally had impressed him less than a dot on a page of Braille. Suddenly, all the pleasure she had been feeling was swamped by a wave of homesickness, a yearning to feel welcomed and loved instead of an unwanted trespasser on the island where Helios and Rhodon had fallen in love.

As if aware of her shrinking withdrawal, Terzan traced a fingertip along the dial of his Braille wristwatch. Hastily, she took the hint, wincing as chair legs grated across the stone-flagged floor.

'We'd better hurry,' she urged stiffly. 'Nikos must be anxious to reach Karios before dark.'

'Nikos is fortunate,' he replied with puzzling obliqueness, 'he is more capable than I of navigating the mysterious unknown. Also,' he clipped with a return to arrogant normality, 'he has been quick to grasp that time means little to one who lives in perpetual darkness. This wristwatch is useful,' his lips twisted wryly, 'but its one great limitation is that when it indicates the hour of twelve there is no way of telling whether it is noon or midnight.'

They had almost reached the gate leading out of the Old Town when he stopped and raised his head, his nostrils twitching.

'Christos . . .!' he exclaimed, a slow smile breaking the solemnity of his features. 'I had almost forgotten his existence.' Obviously guided by a keen sense of smell, he wheeled about to retrace their steps until they halted in front of a shop window when Angie, too, became aware of mingled aromas drifting from an open doorway. A man looked up from his work when they entered and immediately his dark features were lightened by a grin of welcome.

'Terzan, dear old friend . . .!' He leapt across the counter to pump his hand. 'How pleased I am, how delighted to see you deserting your monkish existence on that damned island! Ah . . .!' His dancing eyes alighted upon Angie, attached like a pale butterfly to Terzan's towering shadow. 'You have been quick to revert to normal—aren't you going to introduce me to the lovely creature clinging so fondly to your arm?'

If Terzan was surprised by the description he did not show it, but drew Angie forward to introduce her with a smile.

'Angelina, I should like you to meet Christos Koniaris, whose skill in blending perfumes is excelled only by his expertise in combining charm and flattery. Christos,' he addressed his friend more gravely, 'this is Angelina, my rather shy young wife—do I need to tell you why I have brought her here?'

'Indeed not.' Christos' appreciative, roving glance caused her to blush. 'You have brought her as inspiration for my next masterpiece, an incentive to create a perfume with a scent that must combine the innocence of eyes grey as the plumage of a wild dove and the maturity of a mouth that is no stranger to pain; the delicacy of features drawn with a fine-nibbed pen and a form showing the promise of full-bodied ripeness soon to come.'

Filled with confusion, Angie turned away from eyes that saw too much, that seemed able to define thoughts as yet unexamined, kept secret even from herself.

'Don't allow him to embarrass you, Angelina,' Terzan urged with a smile. 'Simply because a surprising number of credulous women credit his scented love philtres and perfumes with the miraculous power to turn indifferent mates into insatiable lovers his head has been turned, to the extent that he considers himself something of a wizard, fortune-teller, and mind-reading guru all rolled into one.'

'You underestimate me, dear friend!' Christos roared with laughter, yet his dark eyes were sincere when he assured Angie, 'Such silly feminine notions can be discounted, of course, nevertheless it is true that of all the means of self-expression available to women none is more revealing than perfume. By its means, the very soul of woman, her spiritual atmosphere, can be infused into her own personal fragrance. Through perfume, her thoughts can be expressed without the use of a single word. I may be the artist, but it is she alone who provides the tones and overtones, the tints and highlights, the depths and the shallows of her own portrait in perfume.'

'Be that as it may,' Terzan interrupted firmly, 'so far as my wife's perfume is concerned I insist that its predominant scent shall be of roses.'

'I could not agree more,' Christos nodded vigorously. 'No other essence is more stirring to man's aesthetic emotions nor can act as a more refining influence. "The rose distils a healing balm, the beating pulse of pain to calm", eh, Terzan? The name of my new creation shall contain but one word,' he decided with his eyes upon Angie, 'Angelina—the name bestowed by the gods upon their chosen helpmates!'

Much later, filled with an inner trembling that would not be stilled, Angie silently led the way out of the town's precincts with Christos's promise that the perfume would be despatched as soon as possible to Karios still ringing in their ears. Her preoccupation with her thoughts was so intense that she did not notice Terzan's moroseness until he checked her progress, holding her arms captive while he demanded roughly:

'What's wrong now, Angelina? You were reluctant to take from me either clothes or jewellery and flatly refused to accept furs, but surely a gift of perfume cannot offend against your principles? Even in the old days when love affairs were full of romantic passion, respect and love, when courtship was carried out beneath the strict eyes of parents, a gift of perfume was not considered offensive.' Suddenly his fingers bit into her arms,

tight as the lash of words projected through
clenched teeth. 'I may have built up a reputation
of being a hard man in the business world, but
even my worst enemy would have to admit that as
well as insisting upon value for money I have
always been prompt to pay my debts. You have
been extremely ... obliging, *elika*, I owe you
much, why won't you allow me to discharge my
debt?'

'Obliging . . .?' she echoed weakly, fighting a
crazy notion that the ground had suddenly began
to tilt. 'If that's all I've been, then surely a bottle
of perfume is ample exchange for services rendered——'

'Oh, Angelina,' he ground, lowering his head
until his brow was resting upon hers, 'have I hurt
you again, or are you really as cold and uncaring
as you sound? *God!*' he exploded violently. '*How I
wish I could see!*'

But at that moment, standing shocked and cold
as ice, with tears of heartbreak coursing silently
down her cheeks, Angie felt not the least bit guilty
about offering up a prayer of thanks for the small
consolation that he could not.

CHAPTER THIRTEEN

CILLA was not in the least impressed by the shapely dark green bottle filled with perfume that was delivered to Karios two days later. She looked up from the magazine she was scanning with bored, uninterested eyes when Nikos tapped upon the door of a small drawing-room and came in carrying a parcel for Angie.

'What is it?' Cilla queried, her blue eyes sharply avaricious, then when her glance fell upon the name 'Angelina' scrawled in gold letters across the face of the bottle, the elegant sealed stopper, and the nest of satin that was obviously the product of a house of quality, her lips drew into a tight line of displeasure.

'It's a perfume created especially for me by a friend of Terzan's,' Angie sighed, her pleasure in the gift slightly diminished by the reminder of the motive behind the donation. 'He wants me to wear a perfume that's entirely my own, one he'll be able to recognise instantly whenever I walk into his presence.'

But when she unscrewed the stopper and stroked a little of the perfume across her wrist, the faintly sweet yet heady fragrance stirred a delighted response from numbed emotions. 'Oh, how lovely . . .!' She held out her wrist to Cilla, inviting her to sniff. 'Christos truly is a wizard.'

'A psychological genius would be more apt,' Cilla drawled. 'He's captured your personality perfectly with a perfume that conjures up a picture of a great-grandmother dressed in crinoline trimmed with lace, a bonnet tied beneath her chin with ribbons, fingerless mitts, a fan and clouds of attar of roses.'

The sneer drove every vestige of delight from Angie's face. Gravely she regarded her sister, wondering how two people who had once been so close, who since early childhood had shared each other's joys and sorrows, hopes and fears, could have drifted so far apart that they now spoke and acted like strangers. But she had one last secret left to share, a tremendous event which she felt certain would be bound to draw them back into the ring of family harmony that had bound them so tightly together.

'Cilla . . .' She hesitated and swallowed hard.

'Yes, what is it?' With a gesture of irritation Cilla discarded her magazine. The solitude of Karios was getting her down to the extent that any diversion was welcome, even her sister's dull prattling. Curiosity stirred as she noted the rise and fall of colour in Angie's cheeks, the trembling mouth that seemed undecided whether to break into a smile or a quiver, misty eyes that glowed with a light from within, the curvaceous rounding of a hitherto wand-slim body, which altogether added a bloom, a surprisingly lovely maturity to her sister's usually wistful features. A pang of jealousy shot sharpness through her tone when impatiently she snapped, 'If you have something to say then for heaven's sake say it!'

'Sorry,' Angie gulped, brushing a hand across dazed eyes, 'if I appear hesitant it's because I'm finding difficulty saying the words out loud. I think . . . no,' she corrected with a shake of her head, 'I'm almost certain . . .' she drew in a deep, quivering breath, 'that I'm going to have a baby!'

The silence that followed her announcement was so intense that the ticking of a clock in the hallway could plainly be heard. She waited tense as a high note for Cilla's reaction, scanning her shocked, incredulous face for some sign of delight, of concern, or even of resignation to the fact that Terzan, as an expectant father, must now be considered out of bounds. But all she saw was rigid disbelief preceding the dawn of savage anger.

'Devious, calculating cat!' Cilla jumped to her feet, quivering with feline spite, her hands clasping and unclasping as if fighting an impulse to strike.

Angie backed out of reach of pointed, red-tipped fingernails that looked hooked, ready to scar resentment down the length of her cheeks, and gasped a bewildered protest.

'I didn't intend this to happen, nor, I'm certain, did Terzan, but I'm sure he'll accept, as I have—as you must—that whatever regrets we might feel the welfare of the baby must come first.'

'You mean you haven't told him yet?' Cilla grabbed the knowledge like a lifeline. 'Then you mustn't!' she shot when Angie shook her head.

'Why . . .?'

'You dare to ask me that,' Cilla stormed, 'when you're perfectly well aware that Terzan married you on impulse, uncaring which anonymous creature shared his bed once it seemed certain that the one he really loved was unavailable! And now, just when he's on the verge of broaching the subject of divorce, you intend to blackmail him into living the rest of his life with a wife he can barely tolerate and a child he doesn't want.'

'You've discussed divorce with Terzan?' Angie questioned stonily, white to the lips.

'But of course,' Cilla scoffed. 'Our main topic of conversation whenever we're alone is our future happiness, the things we intend to do, the places we intend to go, once he is finally free of you '

'He . . . he doesn't like strange places.' Desperately, Angie tried to convince herself that Cilla was lying. 'I'm the only one he'll trust to act as his guide—he told me so.'

Cilla's laughter rang with chilling triumph. 'Then how is it that you know nothing of the plans afoot? Why has he omitted to tell you that he's even now preparing to leave Karios for an indefinite period?'

'I don't believe you!' Even Cilla felt moved to pity at the sight of Angie's ashen face, but not far enough to miss the chance of furthering her own advantage.

'Then why not find out for yourself—go upstairs and ask Nikos why he's packing Terzan's belongings into suitcases, and at the same time,' she drawled, 'ask Lira why she's doing exactly the same with mine!'

Long after she had followed Cilla's suggestion, Angie sat slumped in her bedroom, painfully nursing her betrayal. Nikos had been unable to supply any information about his master's destination; all he knew, he had told her mournfully, was that he had been ordered to pack sufficient items for a prolonged absence and to instruct Lira that their guest would be leaving at the same time.

'When . . .?' Angie had croaked, humiliated at having been reduced to questioning a servant, even one so loyal as Nikos.

'First thing in the morning,' he had told her, his dark Greek eyes brimming with sympathy, 'just the *kirios* and your sister—it appears that this time even my services will not be required.'

As she sat hugged in misery even the child she was carrying, the tiny spark of life whose existence only Christos had been wise enough to suspect, was forgotten as she dredged her mind for the reason behind Terzan's latest act of treachery.

With a moan of shame she recalled how only the night before he had come to her bedroom—as he had every night of their marriage—attracted like a flame to a moth that put up a fluttering fight, knowing she was destined to succumb to searing passion, to lovemaking that deprived her of every vestige of will, to eyes gleaming bright as a nighttime prowler that devoured her timidity in a blaze of amber.

'*Terzan,*' she had murmured, overcome by tender possessiveness, '*your lashes are so thick they could be used for dusters!*' He had responded by growling a laugh against the hollow of her throat, stirring into eruption a sensuous quake that had shaken the very depths of her hungry body.

The intimacy they had shared, the moments of joy, the pleasure she felt certain had not been hers alone, rendered Cilla's hints unbelievable. That he was ready to leave the island, taking Cilla with him, was no longer in doubt, but there had to be a feasible explanation, she argued desperately, he at least should be given the chance to state in his own words the reason for his departure, instead of being judged on the evidence of a notoriously biased witness!

They had fallen into a routine of working in Terzan's study for a few hours each day, immediately the mail was delivered to the island, so when she glanced out of the window and saw Nikos trudging up to the house from the direction of the jetty with a mailbag slung across his shoulder she sat for a few minutes, concentrating upon calming quivering nerves, then forced herself to walk calmly down to his study.

As quietly as possible she opened the door and sidled inside, having learnt from experience that sudden noises were apt to fray his nerves and consequently his temper. In spite of the physical intimacy that had drawn them as close as two people can be, in other respects Terzan remained reticent, fighting a lone battle with the perils that invaded his darkness, wary in case any appeal for help should lessen his chances of being accepted as normal. But his reaction to an incident that had occurred some weeks ago had helped her to appreciate the strain imposed upon him by his lack of visual warning of imminent sound.

They had been strolling together along the beach when suddenly the calm of the day had been shattered by the high-pitched whine of a jet plane that had descended faster than sound from the heavens and then levelled out over the island with a demoniacal, ear-splitting scream as it passed directly overhead. Terzan had reacted as other people might to the crack of an explosion on a dark, soundless night, jerking rigid, showing white around the mouth, his brow damp with beads of shock . . .

He was seated at his desk, obviously anticipating her arrival. At the sound of her soft footfall his drumming fingers relaxed and when his head lifted she read upon his face an expression of relief.

'Thank you for coming so promptly.' He sounded sombre and very much on edge. 'There is a great deal of correspondence to be dealt with today, but once it is finished you will be allowed a long rest, I promise you.'

Because you won't be here, she thought dully, sinking down into a chair with a pad and pencil at the ready. Realising that he was in no mood to discuss anything other than the business in hand, she concentrated upon transcribing his rapid dictation, pushing all thoughts of desertion and divorce to the back of her mind. But when she had read out the last of the letters and he had finished dictating a reply she glanced up, then went cold all over, sensing from his sudden stillness, his dark frown, that she was about to receive her painful and final dismissal. There was little consolation to be gained from the knowledge that the words he sought did not come easily.

'Before you go, Angelina, there is something I want to tell you.'

When she did not speak, did not so much as stir, he continued quietly, 'I have decided that the time has come when I must relinquish the crutch of familiar routine and recognisable voices and take up the threads of normal life again. Naturally, I feel reluctant to desert the protection of the shell I have built here on Karios, but personal wellbeing has ceased to be my main consideration, for the first time ever I find myself putting the happiness of another person before my own, and since the solution to my problem cannot be found here, I must search elsewhere for an answer, therefore I shall be leaving the island tomorrow . . .'

'I know . . .' Now that the blow had actually fallen it was easier than she had thought to hide her heartbreak behind a barrier of indifference. 'Cilla has already told me.'

'She has?' His voice sharpened. 'But I specifically asked her not to——' He broke off, then had sufficient gall to sound concerned when he continued, 'I had hoped to spare you as much anxiety as possible, but now that you have been made aware of all the facts, tell me, what is your opinion of my decision? Am I right in assuming that the step I am contemplating is essential if we are not both to be condemned to a lifetime of un-happiness?'

Angie struggled to reach a fair conclusion, to set her own unhappiness and the welfare of their unborn child against his right to marry the only girl he had ever loved. From the very beginning he had been honest about the fact that he regarded her as a poor substitute for Cilla, a second-best bride whose skills had helped to fill the gap left by a proficient secretary; who was useful as a guide; whose naïve gullibility had allowed him to exploit her very obliging body. If she were to rant and rave and scream betrayal he could quite justifiably point out that as a lover he had been dominant but never violent, that one word of rejection, one hint of distress would have been sufficient to remove him permanently from her bedroom. Tears of de-spair could not blind her to the fact that the scales of justice were leaning heavily in his favour. As he and Cilla had so rightly concluded, divorce was the only sane and reasonable answer.

She drew in a long silent breath and with her hands clenched tightly in her lap replied as coolly as she was able.

'As usual, Terzan, you seem to have reached the right decision.' She rose to her feet, urging her trembling limbs not to give way beneath her, and managed to gasp a plea, 'All I ask is that the for-malities are concluded with the least possible delay—that you employ a surgeon with a swift, clean scalpel.'

He winced as if struck, whitening before her eyes until the pallor of shock showed pale beneath his tan. Then as she watched, bewildered, his jaw-line tightened, making his words sound run through with steel.

'I thought I knew you well, Angelina, well enough to understand why you feigned illness in order to avoid my company, well enough to understand your reluctance to give yourself to me completely, your insistence upon keeping one tiny part of yourself a secret to everyone but yourself. It was because of this understanding I thought I had that I did not complain about the absence of one involuntary caress, one loving endearment that was not forced from you. Not until this moment had I even begun to suspect that you were capable of being insensitive—even downright callous!'

The accusation was so unjust it left her bereft of words. That his conscience should be uneasy was understandable, no man in the throes of divorcing his wife to replace her with another could expect to be totally devoid of guilt, but his attempt to lay all the blame on her already overburdened shoulders struck her as unforgivable.

'I'm sorry if your conscience is condemning you for a villain, Terzan,' she told him quietly, retreating towards the door. 'I've co-operated as far as I'm able, but if it's absolution you want then you must seek it elsewhere.'

She stopped on her way back to her room to

retrieve the bottle of perfume she had left in the drawing-room. The box was lying on the table where she had left it, but when she lifted the lid she cried out with distress at the sight of a damp patch spreading darkly over the nest of pale green satin. She lifted the bottle from its resting place and felt moisture beneath her fingers, then when she unscrewed the stopper she discovered that the tiny plug she could have sworn she had replaced in the neck of the bottle was missing and perfume was seeping out of the small hole which the plug should have rendered airtight. Annoyed by her own uncharacteristic carelessness, she wiped the bottle dry and caught her breath when a whiff of fragrance teased her nostrils, reminding her of the happy hours she and Terzan had spent in the Old Town, of the tolerant amusement he had shown while she had searched the bazaar for inexpensive presents, of the way his laughter had rung out when, after her first attempt at bargaining, she had carried off a sponge in triumph only to be dismayed by the discovery that identical sponges were selling for half the price on a stall mere steps away.

Had he known even then, she wondered, allowing a sad tear to trickle down her cheek, that their Greek tragedy of a marriage was almost at an end? The marriage that had begun with good luck rain falling on the chapel during their wedding day and had continued stormy, except for intermittent showers of almost unbearable happiness. And if he had, did that explain the aptness of his choice of perfume—the fragrance that drifted from a crushed, mangled rose?

After an abortive search for the missing stopper she carried the bottle up to her room intending to find out whether the plug of the now empty bottle of perfume that Cilla had given her could be used as a stopgap, but as she was searching through a drawer her fingers came into contact with a swathe of tissue paper wrapped around a present she had bought for Terzan and had completely forgotten to give him. Carefully, she unwound the paper and stared down at the gift cupped in the palm of her hand, a butterfly shaped out of onyx, a pale green, delicately veined mineral common to the islands. She traced a finger along the curve of an outspread wing, wondering if it would remind him of the flight of the butterflies he had once loved to watch, deciding to give it to him as a keepsake because she already had a reminder, a part of him from which she could never be divorced, the infinitely precious child she was now carrying. Just the thought of giving birth to Terzan's daughter or son brought a smile of happiness to her lips, a smile that turned to frozen pain when she sauntered across to the window overlooking the garden where Terzan was stretched out on a lounger, seemingly dozing beneath the shade of a tree. As if the tableau had been staged specifically to kill every last vestige of hope in her heart, Cilla appeared, tiptoeing across the grass towards the unsuspecting Terzan. With a confidence born of assurance, she bent down to kiss his cheek, then

with a cry of pain Angie turned away, appalled by
the eager spring of Terzan's body when he grabbed
her close and captured her mouth with a long,
hungry kiss.

For the rest of the day Angie nursed her agony
during solitary walks along the beach, taking care
to rest at intervals in a hidden part of the garden,
skipping lunch altogether because she knew she
would not be able to eat, then finally deciding, as
she dragged her weary body upstairs, that she
would ask for a tray to be sent to her room rather
than submit to the torture of joining Cilla and
Terzan for dinner, forcing them to endure for her
benefit one last evening of polite friendship when
all the time their thoughts would be dwelling on
the happiness tomorrow would bring.

But when, in response to her request, Lira appeared carrying a tray holding a dish of boiled
octopus she knew that even at the risk of depriving
her baby of nourishment she could not eat it.

'Take it away, Lira!' she begged, repelled by the
reminder of a brown, savage octopus being hauled
from the sea, flung sharply to the ground, then
rubbed in a circular movement against the rough
surface of a rock until it exuded a frothy lather
and changed to the pearly grey colour that told
experienced fishermen that it was ready for the
pot. 'I'll have some bread and cheese instead—also
a glass of fresh milk would be nice.'

Lira's knowing smile caused Angie to panic.
Earthy Greek peasants were hard to deceive and
far from reticent, and already she had sensed Cris-

ulla's speculative eyes upon her rounded breasts and faintly curving tummy. It would be disastrous if, at this late stage, one chance remark to Terzan should alert him to the fact that the wife he could barely tolerate was carrying his unwanted child.

'I . . . I've been putting on too much weight lately,' she stated firmly, looking Lira straight in the eye. 'I've decided that from today I shall diet until I am rid of these unwanted pounds.' Much to her relief, Lira's smile faded to a droop of disappointment before she hurried back to the kitchen to tell Crisulla that she had drawn a wrong conclusion.

Consoled by the knowledge that no further threat to Terzan's happiness loomed upon the horizon, Angie prepared for bed, then sat in a chair by a window overlooking the garden until long after midnight, refusing to allow her mind to dwell upon a future devoid of Terzan, contenting herself with making plans for the baby which she had already decided would be brought up in the vicarage to which she intended to return immediately the divorce had been made absolute.

When a slight sound disturbed the silence of the darkened room she did not even bother to turn her head, writing it off as imagination, or perhaps the effect of a cat on a nocturnal prowl of the garden. Shock froze her to immobility when a low voice reached across her shoulder.

'Crisulla tells me that you did not feel well enough to eat downstairs this evening, *elika*, so as I shall probably have left the island before you awaken in the morning I felt I had to find out whether this time your illness is real or purely imaginary.'

Feeling boneless with shock, she rose to her feet and turned round to study a mocking mouth; eyes flickering an amber query from behind a screen of half-closed lashes; a ripple of muscle beneath silk that told her that beneath the dark dressing-gown he was naked, the bare column of throat encircled by a fine gold chain, and a glimpse of brown chest matted with fine black hairs that supplied proof of the notion, a lounging yet alert stance that recalled to mind a sleek well-fed tomcat whose appetite was satiated yet who was nevertheless unable to discard habits formed during a less sybaritic existence when one meal might have had to last a lifetime.

'I'm not ill, just rather tired,' she whispered, backing away from his intimidating presence.

'Too tired even to spend with your husband the last evening before what might be a prolonged separation?' The lightness of his tone was contradicted by bunching fists thrust deep into the pockets of his dressing-gown.

'You had Cilla to keep you company, so I thought I wouldn't be missed,' she stumbled, then countered the menace of a hissed-in breath by continuing hastily, 'But I did get you a present, something to remind you of Karios.'

The confession took him so much by surprise that when she pressed the small butterfly into his palm he seemed at a loss for words, reminding her of a small boy receiving his very first present, wary of showing too much gratitude in case the gift should suddenly be spirited away.

'You bought this for me?' he repeated roughly, running questing fingers along the rim of an out-stretched wing.

'Why sound so surprised?' She forced a quivering laugh. 'It's merely a worthless trinket that I bought in the bazaar, a replica of the creatures you seem to find appealing—fluttering beauties that supply momentary pleasure, that can be easily squashed when they become bothersome, and are plentiful enough to be brushed aside when a more colourful member of the species hovers into view.'

In spite of her resolve to remain calm bitterness had crept into her last words, adding a ring of accusation she regretted.

'*Angelina . . .!*' When he stepped towards her she dodged aside, leaving him stranded, then averted her eyes, unable to bear the proud Greek's look of humiliation.

'You have never done that before,' he accused bleakly, 'at least I don't think you have—but then it is difficult for a blind man to know when he is being bluffed. Tell me, *elika*,' he was perfectly still except for a muscle jerking violently in his cheek, 'what will happen to us if my mission should fail? What if the surgeon's knife should fumble . . .?'

As it seemed highly unlikely that any solicitor he employed would find it difficult to settle a simple divorce action, she replied with puzzlement:

'As you have so much to lose, I'm certain you will engage the best man possible.'

The rustle of her dressing-gown when she moved, the drift of her perfume, was sufficient to indicate her whereabouts. With a speed that was shocking he swooped, pinning her shoulders in a rock-hard clutch.

'My blindness *does* repel you, doesn't it, Angelina? I've suspected all along that you were just pretending that it did not, but now I want the truth. Admit it,' he shook her unmercifully, 'let me hear you put your disgust into words!'

His cruelty broke down the barrier of calm that had helped to preserve her sanity, the pressure of his body aroused a clamouring deep inside that threatened to force her to her knees, begging to be loved. Only the reminder of the kiss he had exchanged with Cilla, the physical hurt that had throbbed within her body since the moment she had learned that they were leaving the island together, helped her to fight a treacherous yearning to collapse into his arms and sob out her heartbreak.

Desperately clutching the lifeline he had thrown her, she sobbed fierce agreement. '*Yes*, your blindness does repel me!' Hysterically she pummelled his chest with her clenched fists and almost screamed out the lie. '*I hate your groping—detest being mauled!*'

CHAPTER FOURTEEN

THOUGH it was high summer the gardens surrounding the villa were an orgy of green. Still, humid air hung above green hollows, not a leaf stirred, not a ripple disturbed the water of the pool in which, when she glanced sideways, Angie could see her face reflected.

She allowed the shawl she was crocheting to slip down into her lap and leant back in her chair, fingers idle, to continue the daydreams that had helped fill many lonely hours while Terzan was away. It seemed incredible that almost three months should have passed without a letter nor even a hastily scribbled postcard. In an effort not to brood, to strive for a contented state of mind for the sake of their baby, she had kept herself busy crocheting tiny garments, running up simple, loose sundresses on an ancient sewing machine a delighted Crisulla had unearthed once nature had begun supplying proof that her instinct had not been wrong when it had told her that the young *Anghlika* was an expectant mother.

Angie stirred, closed her eyes, and turned a serene yet haunted face towards the sun. She was not yet enormous, indeed, when seated, with a loose smock billowing around her form, she looked very much as normal. It was not until she rose to her feet that the burden she was carrying became obvious. Nevertheless, she was discovering that she needed to sleep each day, so she had taken to napping in the garden so that her baby could derive as much benefit as possible from clean, sweet air and hot Greek sunshine before they were forced to leave for England.

She was just on the verge of dozing off when the crunch of footsteps on a stone-paved path brought an indulgent smile to her lips. From the moment the news of her pregnancy had been made public Nikos had decided that it was his duty to act as her protector in the *kirios*'s absence—a role that set the emotional Greek seesawing between the pride of a crowing cockerel and the anxiety of a mother hen. Angie lifted one drowsy eyelid, wondering what form of refreshment he had fetched this time, and saw him hovering with a tray containing a glass of milk and a few *baclavas*, nutty sweetmeats rich and sticky with honey.

'*Sigha* . . .!' He pleaded with her to take things easy as he deposited the tray on a table placed close to her hand. He beamed, then subconsciously tensed as he waited for the question that sounded less casual with each passing day.

'Has any mail arrived for me yet, Nikos?'

'Not yet,' he admitted gruffly, then attempted to lighten the solemnity of her eyes by observing, 'but there is a boat on the horizon that seems to be heading towards the island, so perhaps . . .' His shoulders lifted in a shrug, indicating that she might hope—but not too much. When her lashes drooped to hide the sparkle of tears he started towards her and, inwardly condemning the *kirios* four times to hell, tried to justify his absence.

'A great deal of work must have accumulated while the *kirios* was in hospital, so doubtless he has once again become embroiled in affairs of business. He will return soon, I am certain, for never has he absented himself so long from the island.'

'How long was he in hospital, Nikos?' Angie reached out an unsteady hand for the glass of milk and started to sip it slowly.

'Many weeks,' he brooded, 'weeks during which the doctors gave him hope but no promises. All the time the surgeons worked on his eyes he never complained of pain or discomfort because always he was hoping for a miracle. But after many painful corneal grafts had failed to take he seemed to lose hope completely, to resign himself to living the life of a blind man.'

'*He* gave up hope?' Her head jerked upright. 'But what about the specialists, what did they have to say?'

'They wanted to make one last attempt to restore his sight in a way that had never been tried before, but he would have none of it,' Nikos sighed. 'From the very beginning he showed a marked distaste for the grafting operation, it was as if not only physically but spiritually he was rejecting spare-part surgery.'

'Second best,' Angie murmured almost to herself. 'He would want nothing that was not entirely of his own choosing.'

'And nothing is exactly what he has been left with,' Nikos's quick ears had caught her words. 'Because of his stubborn independence he has been left blind to the unhappiness he has caused, even blind to the fact that the mistress of Karios bears him a child!'

She ought to have prepared him for the shock of discovering that she was not to be mistress of Karios much longer, but instead she took refuge in cowardice, and intimated that she was tired by leaning back her head and closing her eyes.

He was quick to take the hint. 'Try to sleep,' he encouraged. 'The boat I saw earlier has almost reached the jetty—if it brings mail, I will fetch it to you immediately.'

She took his advice and drifted into a doze, but after what could have been minutes or even half an hour she heard once more the sound of approaching footsteps and jerked wide awake, expecting to see Nikos bringing a letter. But the figure that was approaching with the sun behind him was too tall, too pantherish in stride, to be mistaken for the stockily-built servant.

She did not question the confidence, the sureness of step that directed Terzan straight towards her, because her love for him was so great that, had she been a blinkered bird, she knew she could have homed directly to him. With her heart in her eyes she faced the stare of smoky lenses, scoured his face and noted that it was so much paler, so much more strained than it had been when she had last seen him. Giving joy full rein because there was no danger of detection, she whispered, 'Terzan . . .!' his name brushing soft as the wing of a butterfly passed her lips.

An age seemed to pass before he responded, an age of tense uncertainty during which dark lenses bore down upon her face, steady and intently probing.

'Angelina,' he finally rasped, 'now that I am home, you seem in no hurry to learn the outcome of my journey. Don't you care,' he clamped, 'have you no interest at all in what has been happening?'

The sharpness of his voice jolted her back to painful reality. Remaining still and cold as a statue, her head a drooping silver bell, she forced the reply.

'I felt there was no need to ask, you always manage to accomplish whatever you set out to do, Terzan, so I'm sure you've managed to get a divorce.'

'*Divorce . . .?*' Suddenly he dropped to his knees beside her and whipped dark glasses away from blazing amber eyes. 'What are you saying, Angelina?'

'Cilla told me you were leaving the island to seek a divorce so that you and she could marry,' she gasped, terrified by his look of anger.

'*May she go ten times to hell!*' he spat, tightening his fists in a spasm of impotent fury. 'I made it worth your sister's while to leave Karios because I suspected her of plotting mischief, but I had no idea that I had left it too late!'

Angie sat dazed, wondering if she were dreaming, if Nikos would suddenly arrive to shake her awake, but when Terzan gripped her shoulders the pain was too real, the tremors that ran through her body too agonisingly familiar.

'Then why did you leave?' she choked. 'What reason did you have for going away?'

The flame in his eyes died low. He hesitated to steady his voice before reminding her huskily, 'The surgeon's scalpel, remember, Angelina . . .?' He waited for some sign of comprehension, then when she did not speak he spelled out gravely, 'Priscilla knew that it was my intention to return to the hospital for further treatment on my eyes. One last attempt, the surgeons said, might restore my sight, and though I had decided I had had enough of unsuccessful operations, of having my hopes built up and then having them dashed, the chance that you might not shrink from me if I were sighted, that you might even be able to love me, was sufficient incentive to make me change my mind. For four days after the bandages were removed I was convinced the operation had failed, even though the doctors assured me that with eye operations one can never expect immediate results, then gradually I began to get a very misty vision of the world—the first object I was able to identify was the small onyx butterfly that never left my possession, that gave me courage to go through with the operation.'

She stared transfixed by eyes she had imagined were blind, then when comprehension fully dawned a slow, painful blush began rising in her cheeks.

'Are you telling me that you can see?' she trembled, lifting her hands up to her face as if compelled to hide.

'I can see perfectly.' He stared deeply at her stricken face, then questioned softly, 'Shall I tell you what I can see? I see a face that is a perfect match for a gentle, lovely voice; I see eyes tender and grey as dove-down; I see a blush that recalls to mind a painfully shy young bride and a mouth——' Suddenly his composure broke. 'Oh, that *mouth*, Angelina!' he groaned, pulling her into his arms. 'I have recaptured its sweetness in my dreams, I have ached for its loving generous blessing every waking moment . . .!'

Questions, pleas, explanations were all thrust aside by the impatient Greek who could wait no longer. She was crushed, entwined tightly within his arms, and kissed until he had slaked his thirst for sweetness, but when her impassioned responses threatened to stampede his desire for more, he stamped a brake upon passion and held her very still.

'I adore you, *elika*,' he swore hoarsely. 'All that I am is yours to do with as you will, so why do you hold back, where do I find the key to that secret store of reserve?'

She did not pretend to misunderstand. 'I love you very much, Terzan,' she told him shakily, 'but trust takes time—just a short while ago you were in love with Cilla—I saw you kissing her the night before you left the island.'

He released her to cup her small pointed chin between his palms. 'I thought I was kissing you,' he told her simply. 'Only moments before I had chided you for your coolness, so when I smelled your perfume and felt the touch of lips against my cheek I imagined it was your way of showing penitence. Also,' his voice hardened, 'I never loved Priscilla—it amused me for a while to pander to her conceit and to play up to the notions of her stupid friends who seemed to think she was a siren who could entice any man she wanted into her net.'

'But the letters you wrote,' she protested, 'the threats you made when she refused to marry you?'

'Were a punishment,' he drawled, showing a hint of ruthless Greek. 'I was appalled by the effect her callous rejection might have had on any man in my position who was genuinely in love. I could have not been more dismayed when I received a message informing me that a Miss Rose was waiting to be picked up at the airport.'

When, with eyes softly glowing, Angie stood on tiptoe to beg forgiveness with a kiss his hands snapped down to her waist, then suddenly froze.

'There is something different about you,' he frowned, then closed his eyes, using his hands to explore in Braille. The impact of his discovery shocked his eyes wide open to decipher truth from her sweet confusion.

'My wife shall be as fruitful as the vine. My children like olive plants around my table?' He phrased the shaken quotation like a question, and when shyly she nodded he drew her into his arms, cradling her closely until she felt cherished. 'Sweet Angel bride,' his lips burrowed into the soft curve of his throat so that his passionate words mingled with the tears that no Greek male is ever ashamed to shed, 'forgive me for the torment I have imposed upon you. If you will allow me, I swear I will spend the rest of my life trying to make amends.'

'Please don't, my darling,' her attempt to tease was weakened by a great depth of emotion. 'Why waste time learning repentance when you are so expert at making love?'

Momentarily, she felt him tense. 'Does that mean that you no longer mind being *mauled*?'

Though the words were muffled his pain was unmistakable, and with a distressed cry she tightened her arms around him to assure him vehemently, 'I *lied* to you, Terzan!'

'Twice,' he reminded her sternly, lifting his head to display a glow in his eyes that told her she was forgiven. 'You also implied that your perfect little face was plain. Once, Nikos likened you to a tightly furled rosebud tantalising with hidden promise. Blindness restricted me to knowing only your sweet inner fragrance, but now, *elika*,' heat rushed to her cheeks as she was bathed in the glow of rapidly-kindling flame, 'I can't wait to lose myself in the scent, sight and touch of an enchanting flower, my delightfully blossoming Angelina Rose.'

Take these 4 best-selling novels FREE

ANNE HAMPSON
gates of steel

ANNE MATHER
sweet revenge

VIOLET WINSPEAR
devil in a silver room

JANET DAILEY
no quarter asked